POCKET

HEART OF DARKNESS

In this remarkable novelette, Conrad draws from his own experiences to create two striking characters whose struggles with the brooding evil and misery of colonial Africa reveal man's vulnerability to as well as ultimate triumph over the forces of greed and temptation. Here, in the rich prose of a master of the English language, is a story of great significance to the modern reader.

The Reader's Supplement to this ENRICHED CLASSICS edition appears in the center insert. It has been prepared under the supervision of an editorial committee directed by Harry Shefter, Professor of English, New York University, and author of many books used extensively for the improvement of skills in the language arts. The contributing editors for this edition were Leonard R. N. Ashley, Professor of English, Brooklyn College, and Aaron Traister, Professor of English, New York University. Grateful acknowledgment is made to the Picture Collection Division of the New York Public Library which provided much of the illustrative material.

POCKET

Heart of Darkness

Joseph Conrad

AN ENRICHED CLASSIC/PUBLISHED BY POCKET BOOKS

ACKNOWLEDGMENTS

Etching of Joseph Conrad by Muirhead Bone. Reprinted by permission of J. M. Dent & Sons Ltd., Publishers, and the Trustees of the Joseph Conrad Estate.

"Rotherhithe Wapping," by James McNeill Whistler, 1860. Bibliothèque Nationale, Paris. Reprinted with permission.

"A secretary knitting during a lull," by R. F. Shabelitz, published in *Harper's Weekly*, May 1, 1909. Reprinted with permission.

"Natives with improvised litter." Photograph by Eleanor de Cheteint. Reprinted with permission.

"Shrunken head of a Yumbo." From *Faces of Bronze*, published by Universe Books Inc., New York.

CHAPTER
1

The *Nellie*, a cruising yawl, swung to her anchor without a flutter of the sails, and was at rest. The flood had made, the wind was nearly calm, and being bound down the river, the only thing for it was to come to and wait for the turn of the tide.

The sea-reach of the Thames stretched before us like the beginning of an interminable waterway. In the offing the sea and the sky were welded together without a joint, and in the luminous space the tanned sails of the barges drifting up with the tide seemed to stand still in red clusters of canvas sharply peaked, with gleams of varnished sprits. A haze rested on the low shores that ran out to sea in vanishing flatness. The air was dark above Gravesend, and farther back still seemed condensed into a mournful gloom, brooding motionless over the biggest, and the greatest, town on earth.

The Director of Companies was our captain and our host. We four affectionately watched his back as he stood in the bows looking to seaward. On the whole river there was nothing that looked half so nautical. He resembled a pilot, which to a seaman is trustworthiness personified. It was difficult to realize his work was not out there in the luminous estuary, but behind him, within the brooding gloom.

Between us there was, as I have already said somewhere, the bond of the sea. Besides holding our hearts together through long periods of separation, it had the effect of making us tolerant of each other's yarns—and even convictions. The Lawyer—the best of old fellows —had, because of his many years and many virtues, the only cushion on deck, and was lying on the only rug. The Accountant had brought out already a box of dominoes, and was toying architecturally with the bones. Marlow sat cross-legged right aft, leaning against the mizzen-mast. He had sunken cheeks, a yellow complexion, a straight back, an ascetic aspect, and, with his arms dropped, the palms of hands outwards, resembled an idol. The director, satisfied the anchor had good hold, made his way aft and sat down amongst us. We exchanged a few words lazily. Afterwards there was silence on board the yacht. For some reason or other we did not begin that game of dominoes. We felt meditative, and fit for nothing but placid staring. The day was ending in a serenity of still and exquisite brilliance. The water shone pacifically; the sky, without a speck, was a benign immensity of unstained light; the very mist on the Essex marshes was like a gauzy and radiant fabric, hung from the wooded rises inland, and draping the low shores in diaphanous folds. Only the gloom to the west, brooding over the upper reaches, became more sombre every minute, as if angered by the approach of the sun.

And at last, in its curved and imperceptible fall, the sun sank low, and from glowing white changed to a dull red without rays and without heat, as if about to go out suddenly, stricken to death by the touch of that gloom brooding over a crowd of men.

Forthwith a change came over the waters, and the serenity became less brilliant but more profound. The old river in its broad reach rested unruffled at the decline of day, after ages of good service done to the race that peopled its banks, spread out in the tranquil dignity of a waterway leading to the uttermost ends of the earth. We looked at the venerable stream not in the vivid flush of a short day that comes and departs for ever, but in the august light of abiding memories. And indeed nothing is easier for a man who has, as the phrase goes, "followed the sea" with reverence and affection, than to evoke the great spirit of the past upon the lower reaches of the Thames. The tidal current runs to and fro in its unceasing service, crowded with memories of men and ships it had borne to the rest of home or to the battles of the sea. It had known and served all the men of whom the nation is proud, from Sir Francis Drake to Sir John Franklin, knights all, titled and untitled—the great knights-errant of the sea. It had borne all the ships whose names are like jewels flashing in the night of time, from the *Golden Hind* returning with her round flanks full of treasure, to be visited by the Queen's Highness and thus pass

out of the gigantic tale, to the *Erebus* and *Terror,*
bound on other conquests—and that never returned. It
had known the ships and the men. They had sailed
from Deptford, from Greenwich, from Erith—the ad-
venturers and the settlers; kings' ships and the ships of
men on 'Change; captains, admirals, the dark "interlopers" of the Eastern trade, the commissioned "gen-
erals" of East India fleets. Hunters for gold or pursuers
of fame, they all had gone out on that stream, bearing
the sword, and often the torch, messengers of the might
within the land, bearers of a spark from the sacred fire.
What greatness had not floated on the ebb of that river
into the mystery of an unknown earth! . . . The dreams
of men, the seed of commonwealths, the germs of em-
pires.

The sun set; the dusk fell on the stream, and lights
began to appear along the shore. The Chapman light-
house, a three-legged thing erect on a mud-flat, shone
strongly. Lights of ships moved in the fairway—a great
stir of lights going up and going down. And farther
west on the upper reaches the place of the monstrous
town was still marked ominously on the sky, a brooding
gloom in sunshine, a lurid glare under the stars.

"And this also," said Marlow suddenly, "has been one
of the dark places on the earth."

He was the only man of us who still "followed the
sea." The worst that could be said of him was that he
did not represent his class. He was a seaman, but he
was a wanderer, too, while most seamen lead, if one
may so express it, a sedentary life. Their minds are of
the stay-at-home order, and their home is always with
them—the ship; and so is their country—the sea. One
ship is very much like another, and the sea is always

the same. In the immutability of their surroundings the foreign shores, the foreign faces, the changing immensity of life, glide past, veiled not by a sense of mystery but a slightly disdainful ignorance; for there is nothing mysterious to a seaman unless it be the sea itself, which is the mistress of his existence and as inscrutable as Destiny. For the rest, after his hours of work, a casual stroll or a casual spree on shore suffices to unfold for him the secret of a whole continent, and generally he finds the secret not worth knowing. The yarns of seamen have a direct simplicity, the whole meaning of which lies within the shell of a cracked nut. But Marlow was not typical (if his propensity to spin yarns be excepted) and to him the meaning of an episode was not inside like a kernel but outside, enveloping the tale which brought it out only as a glow brings out a haze, in the likeness of one of these misty halos that sometimes are made visible by the spectral illumination of moonshine.

His remark did not seem at all surprising. It was just like Marlow. It was accepted in silence. No one took the trouble to grunt even; and presently he said, very slow—

"I was thinking of very old times, when the Romans first came here, nineteen hundred years ago—the other day. . . . Light came out of this river since—you say Knights? Yes; but it is like a running blaze on a plain, like a flash of lightning in the clouds. We live in the flicker—may it last as long as the old earth keeps rolling! But darkness was here yesterday. Imagine the feelings of a commander of a fine—what d'ye call 'em? —trireme in the Mediterranean, ordered suddenly to the north; run overland across the Gauls in a hurry; put in charge of one of these craft the legionaries—a wonderful lot of handy men they must have been, too—used to build, apparently by the hundred, in a month or two, if we may believe what we read. Imagine him here—the very end of the world, a sea the colour of lead, a sky the colour of smoke, a kind of ship about as rigid as a concertina—and going up this river with stores, or orders, or what you like. Sand-banks, marshes, forests, savages,—precious little to eat fit for a civilized man, nothing but Thames water to drink. No Falernian wine here, no going ashore. Here and there a military camp lost in a wilderness, like a needle in a bundle of hay—cold, fog, tempests, disease, exile, and death,—death skulking in the air, in the water, in the bush. They must have been dying like flies here. Oh, yes—he did it. Did it very well, too, no doubt, and without thinking much about it either, except afterwards to brag of what he had gone through in his time, perhaps. They were men enough to face the darkness. And perhaps he was cheered by keeping his eye on a chance of promotion to a fleet at Ravenna by and by, if he had good friends in Rome and survived the awful climate. Or think of a decent young citizen in a toga—perhaps too much dice, you know—coming out here in the train of some prefect, or tax-gatherer, or trader even, to mend his fortunes. Land in a swamp, march through the woods, and in some inland post feel the savagery, the utter savagery, had closed round him,—all that mysterious life of the wilderness that stirs in the forest, in the jungles, in the hearts of wild men. There's no initiation either into such mysteries. He has to live in the midst of the incomprehensible, which is also detestable. And it has a fascination, too, that goes

to work upon him. The fascination of the abomination
—you know, imagine the growing regrets, the longing
to escape, the powerless disgust, the surrender, the
hate."

He paused.

"Mind," he began again, lifting one arm from the
elbow, the palm of the hand outwards, so that, with his
legs folded before him, he had the pose of a Buddha
preaching in European clothes and without a lotus-
flower—"Mind, none of us would feel exactly like this.
What saves us is efficiency—the devotion to efficiency.
But these chaps were not much account, really. They
were no colonists; their administration was merely a
squeeze, and nothing more, I suspect. They were con-
querors, and for that you want only brute force—
nothing to boast of, when you have it, since your
strength is just an accident arising from the weakness
of others. They grabbed what they could get for the
sake of what was to be got. It was just robbery with
violence, aggravated murder on a great scale, and men
going at it blind—as is very proper for those who tackle
a darkness. The conquest of the earth, which mostly
means the taking it away from those who have a
different complexion or slightly flatter noses than ourselves, is not a pretty thing when you look into it too
much. What redeems it is the idea only. An idea at the
back of it; not a sentimental pretence but an idea; and
an unselfish belief in the idea—something you can set
up, and bow down before, and offer a sacrifice to. . . ."

He broke off. Flames glided in the river, small green
flames, red flames, white flames, pursuing, overtaking,
joining, crossing each other—then separating slowly or
hastily. The traffic of the great city went on in the deep-

ening night upon the sleepless river. We looked on, waiting patiently—there was nothing else to do till the end of the flood; but it was only after a long silence, when he said, in a hesitating voice, "I suppose you fellows remember I did once turn fresh-water sailor for a bit," that we knew we were fated, before the ebb began to run, to hear about one of Marlow's inconclusive experiences.

"I don't want to bother you much with what happened to me personally," he began, showing in this remark the weakness of many tellers of tales who seem so often unaware of what their audience would best like to hear; "yet to understand the effect of it on me you ought to know how I got out there, what I saw, how I went up that river to the place where I first met the poor chap. It was the farthest point of navigation and the culminating point of my experience. It seemed somehow to throw a kind of light on everything about me—and into my thoughts. It was sombre enough, too— and pitiful—not extraordinary in any way—not very clear either. No, not very clear. And yet it seemed to throw a kind of light.

"I had then, as you remember, just returned to London after a lot of Indian Ocean, Pacific, China Seas—a regular dose of the East—six years or so, and I was loafing about, hindering you fellows in your work and invading your homes, just as though I had got a heavenly mission to civilize you. It was very fine for a time, but after a bit I did get tired of resting. Then I began to look for a ship—I should think the hardest work on earth. But the ships wouldn't even look at me. And I got tired of that game, too.

"Now when I was a little chap I had a passion for

maps. I would look for hours at South America, or Africa, or Australia, and lose myself in all the glories of exploration. At that time there were many blank spaces on the earth, and when I saw one that looked particularly inviting on a map (but they all look that) I would put my finger on it and say, When I grow up I will go there. The North Pole was one of these places, I remember. Well, I haven't been there yet, and shall not try now. The glamour's off. Other places were scattered about the Equator, and in every sort of latitude all over the two hemispheres. I have been in some of them, and . . . well, we won't talk about that. But there was one yet—the biggest, the most blank, so to speak—that I had a hankering after.

"True, by this time it was not a blank space any more. It had got filled since my boyhood with rivers and lakes and names. It had ceased to be a blank space of delightful mystery—a white patch for a boy to dream gloriously over. It had become a place of darkness. But there was in it one river especially, a mighty big river, that you could see on the map, resembling an immense snake uncoiled, with its head in the sea, its body at rest curving afar over a vast country, and its tail lost in the depths of the land. And as I looked at the map of it in a shop-window, it fascinated me as a snake would a bird—a silly little bird. Then I remembered there was a big concern, a Company for trade on that river. Dash it all! I thought to myself, they can't trade without using some kind of craft on that lot of fresh water—steamboats! Why shouldn't I try to get charge of one? I went on along Fleet Street, but could not shake off the idea. The snake had charmed me.

"You understand it was a Continental concern, that

Trading society; but I have a lot of relations living on the Continent, because it's cheap and not so nasty as it looks, they say.

"I am sorry to own I began to worry them. This was already a fresh departure for me. I was not used to get things that way, you know. I always went my own road and on my own legs where I had a mind to go. I wouldn't have believed it of myself; but, then—you see —I felt somehow I must get there by hook or by crook. So I worried them. The men said 'My dear fellow,' and did nothing. Then—would you believe it?—I tried the women. I, Charlie Marlow, set the women to work—to get a job. Heavens! Well, you see, the notion drove me. I had an aunt, a dear enthusiastic soul. She wrote: 'It will be delightful. I am ready to do anything, anything for you. It is a glorious idea. I know the wife of a very high personage in the Administration, and also a man who has lots of influence with,' etc., etc. She was determined to make no end of fuss to get me appointed skipper of a river steamboat, if such was my fancy.

"I got my appointment—of course; and I got it very quick. It appears the Company had received news that one of their captains had been killed in a scuffle with the natives. This was my chance, and it made me the more anxious to go. It was only months and months afterwards, when I made the attempt to recover what was left of the body, that I heard the original quarrel arose from a misunderstanding about some hens. Yes, two black hens. Fresleven—that was the fellow's name, a Dane—thought himself wronged somehow in the bargain, so he went ashore and started to hammer the chief of the village with a stick. Oh, it didn't surprise me in the least to hear this, and at the same time to be told that Fresleven was the gentlest, quietest creature that ever walked on two legs. No doubt he was; but he had been a couple of years already out there engaged in the noble cause, you know, and he probably felt the need at last of asserting his self-respect in some way. Therefore he whacked the old nigger mercilessly, while a big crowd of his people watched him, thunderstruck, till some man—I was told the chief's son—in desperation at hearing the old chap yell, made a tentative jab with a spear at the white man—and of course it went quite easy between the shoulder-blades. Then the whole population cleared into the forest, expecting all kinds of calamities to happen, while, on the other hand, the steamer Fresleven commanded left also in a bad panic, in charge of the engineer, I believe. Afterwards nobody seemed to trouble much about Fresleven's remains, till I got out and stepped into his shoes. I couldn't let it rest, though; but when an opportunity offered at last to meet my predecessor, the grass growing through his ribs was tall enough to hide his bones. They were all there. The supernatural being had not been touched after he fell. And the village was deserted, the huts gaped black, rotting, all askew within the fallen enclosures. A calamity had come to it, sure enough. The people had vanished. Mad terror had scattered them, men, women, and children, through the bush, and they had never returned. What became of the hens I don't know either. I should think the cause of progress got them, anyhow. However, through this glorious affair I got my appointment, before I had fairly begun to hope for it.

"I flew around like mad to get ready, and before forty-eight hours I was crossing the Channel to show myself to my employers, and sign the contract. In a very few hours I arrived in a city that always makes me think of a whited sepulchre. Prejudice no doubt. I had no difficulty in finding the Company's offices. It was the biggest thing in the town, and everybody I met was full of it. They were going to run an over-sea empire, and make no end of coin by trade.

"A narrow and deserted street in deep shadow, high houses, innumerable windows with venetian blinds, a dead silence, grass sprouting between the stones, imposing carriage archways right and left, immense double doors standing ponderously ajar. I slipped through one of these cracks, went up a swept and ungarnished staircase, as arid as a desert, and opened the first door I came to. Two women, one fat and the other slim, sat on straw-bottomed chairs, knitting black wool. The slim one got up and walked straight at me—still knitting with downcast eyes—and only just as I began to think of getting out of her way, as you would for a somnambulist, stood still, and looked up. Her dress was as plain as an umbrella-cover, and she turned round without a word and preceded me into a waiting-room. I gave my name, and looked about. Deal table in the middle, plain chairs all round the walls, on one end a large shining map, marked with all the colours of a rainbow. There was a vast amount of red—good to see at any time, because one knows that some real work is done in there, a deuce of a lot of blue, a little green, smears of orange, and, on the East Coast, a purple patch, to show where the jolly pioneers of progress drink the jolly lager-beer. However, I wasn't going into any of these. I was going into the yellow. Dead in the centre. And the river was there—fascinating—deadly—like a snake. Ough! A door opened, a white-haired secretarial head, but wearing a compassionate expression, appeared, and a skinny forefinger beckoned me into the sanctuary. Its light was dim, and a heavy writing-desk squatted in the middle. From behind that structure came out an impression of pale plumpness in a frock-coat. The great man himself. He was five feet six, I should judge, and had his grip on the handle-end of ever so many millions. He shook hands, I fancy, murmured vaguely, was satisfied with my French. *Bon voyage.*

"In about forty-five seconds I found myself again in the waiting-room with the compassionate secretary, who, full of desolation and sympathy, made me sign some document. I believe I undertook amongst other things not to disclose any trade secrets. Well, I am not going to.

"I began to feel slightly uneasy. You know I am not used to such ceremonies, and there was something ominous in the atmosphere. It was just as though I had been let into some conspiracy—I don't know—something not quite right; and I was glad to get out. In the outer room the two women knitted black wool feverishly. People were arriving, and the younger one was walking back and forth introducing them. The old one sat on her chair. Her flat cloth slippers were propped up on a foot-warmer, and a cat reposed on her lap. She wore a starched white affair on her head, had a wart on one cheek, and silver-rimmed spectacles hung on the tip of her nose. She glanced at me above the glasses. The swift and indifferent placidity of that look troubled me. Two youths with foolish and cheery countenances were being piloted over, and she threw at them the same quick glance of unconcerned wisdom. She seemed to know all about them and about me, too. An eerie feeling came over me. She seemed uncanny and fateful. Often far away there I thought of these two, guarding the door of Darkness, knitting black wool as for a warm pall, one introducing, introducing continuously to the unknown, the other scrutinizing the cheery and foolish faces with unconcerned old eyes. *Ave!* Old knitter of black wool. *Morituri te salutant.* Not many of those she looked at ever saw her again —not half, by a long way.

"There was yet a visit to the doctor. 'A simple formality,' assured me the secretary, with an air of taking an immense part in all my sorrows. Accordingly a young chap wearing his hat over the left eyebrow, some clerk I suppose,—there must have been clerks in the business, though the house was as still as a house in a city of the dead—came from somewhere up-stairs, and led me forth. He was shabby and careless, with ink-stains on the sleeves of his jacket, and his cravat was large and bilowy, under a chin shaped like the toe of an old boot. It was a little too early for the doctor, so I proposed a drink, and thereupon he developed a vein of joviality. As we sat over our vermouths he glorified the Company's business, and by and by I expressed casually my surprise at him not going out there. He became very cool and collected all at once. 'I am not such a fool as I look, quoth Plato to his disciples,' he said sententiously, emptied his glass with great resolution, and we rose.

"The old doctor felt my pulse, evidently thinking of something else the while. 'Good, good for there,' he mumbled, and then with a certain eagerness asked me whether I would let him measure my head. Rather surprised, I said Yes, when he produced a thing like calipers and got the dimensions back and front and every way, taking notes carefully. He was an unshaven little man in a threadbare coat like a gaberdine, with his feet in slippers, and I thought him a harmless fool. 'I always ask leave, in the interests of science, to measure the crania of those going out there,' he said. 'And when they come back, too?' I asked. 'Oh, I never see them,' he remarked; 'and, moreover, the changes take place inside, you know.' He smiled, as if at some quiet joke. 'So you are going out there. Famous. Interesting, too.' He gave me a searching glance, and made another note. 'Ever any madness in your family?' he asked, in a matter-of-fact tone. I felt very annoyed. 'Is that question in the interests of science, too?' 'It would be,' he said, without taking notice of my irritation, 'interesting for science to watch the mental changes of individuals, on the spot, but . . .' 'Are you an alienist?' I interrupted. 'Every doctor should be—a little,' answered that original, imperturbably. 'I have a little theory which you Messieurs who go out there must help me to prove. This is my share in the advantages my country shall reap from the possession of such a magnificent dependency. The mere wealth I leave to others. Pardon my questions, but you are the first Englishman coming under my observation . . .' I hastened to assure him I was not in the least typical. 'If I were,' said I, 'I wouldn't be talking like this to you.' 'What you say is rather profound, and probably erroneous,' he said, with a little laugh. 'Avoid irritation more than exposure to the sun. Adieu. How do you English say, eh? Good-bye. Ah! Good-bye. Adieu. In the tropics one must before

everything keep calm.' . . . He lifted a warning forefinger. . . . '*Du calme, du calme. Adieu.*'

"One thing more remained to do—say good-bye to
my excellent aunt. I found her triumphant. I had a
cup of tea—the last decent cup of tea for many days—
and in a room that most soothingly looked just as you
would expect a lady's drawing-room to look, we had
a long quiet chat by the fireside. In the course of these
confidences it became quite plain to me I had been
represented to the wife of the high dignitary, and goodness knows to how many more people besides, as an
exceptional and gifted creature—a piece of good for-
tune for the Company—a man you don't get hold of
every day. Good heavens! and I was going to take
charge of a two-penny-half-penny river-steamboat with
a penny whistle attached! It appeared, however, I was
also one of the Workers, with a capital—you know.
Something like an emissary of light, something like a
lower sort of apostle. There had been a lot of such rot
let loose in print and talk just about that time, and the
excellent woman, living right in the rush of all that
humbug, got carried off her feet. She talked about
'weaning those ignorant millions from their horrid
ways,' till, upon my word, she made me quite uncom-
fortable. I ventured to hint that the Company was run
for profit.

" 'You forget, dear Charlie, that the labourer is
worthy of his hire,' she said, brightly. It's queer how
out of touch with truth women are. They live in a
world of their own, and there has never been anything like it, and never can be. It is too beautiful altogether, and if they were to set it up it would go to
pieces before the first sunset. Some confounded fact we

men have been living contentedly with ever since the day of creation would start up and knock the whole thing over.

"After this I got embraced, told to wear flannel, be sure to write often, and so on—and I left. In the street—I don't know why—a queer feeling came to me that I was an imposter. Odd thing that I, who used to clear out for any part of the world at twenty-four hours' notice, with less thought than most men give to the crossing of a street, had a moment—I won't say of hesitation, but of startled pause, before this common-place affair. The best way I can explain it to you is by saying that, for a second or two, I felt as though, instead of going to the centre of a continent, I were about to set off for the centre of the earth.

"I left in a French steamer, and she called in every blamed port they have out there, for, as far as I could see, the sole purpose of landing soldiers and custom-house officers. I watched the coast. Watching a coast as it slips by the ship is like thinking about an enigma. There it is before you—smiling, frowning, inviting, grand, mean, insipid, or savage, and always mute with an air of whispering, Come and find out. This one was almost featureless, as if still in the making, with an aspect of monotonous grimness. The edge of a colossal jungle, so dark-green as to be almost black, fringed with white surf, ran straight, like a ruled line, far, far away along a blue sea whose glitter was blurred by a creeping mist. The sun was fierce, the land seemed to glisten and drip with steam. Here and there grayish-whitish specks showed up clustered inside the white surf, with a flag flying above them perhaps. Settlements some centuries old, and still no bigger than pinheads

on the untouched expanse of their background. We
pounded along, stopped, landed soldiers; went on,
landed custom-house clerks to levy toll in what looked
like a God-forsaken wilderness, with a tin shed and a
flag-pole lost in it; landed more soldiers—to take care
of the custom-house clerks, presumably. Some, I heard,
got drowned in the surf; but whether they did or not,
nobody seemed particularly to care. They were just
flung out there, and on we went. Every day the coast
looked the same, as though we had not moved; but
we passed various places—trading places—with names
like Gran' Bassam, Little Popo; names that seemed to
belong to some sordid farce acted in front of a sinister
back-cloth. The idleness of a passenger, my isolation
amongst all these men with whom I had no point of
contact, the oily and languid sea, the uniform sombre-
ness of the coast, seemed to keep me away from the
truth of things, within the toil of a mournful and
senseless delusion. The voice of the surf heard now and
then was a positive pleasure, like the speech of a
brother. It was something natural, that had its reason,
that had a meaning. Now and then a boat from the
shore gave one a momentary contact with reality. It
was paddled by black fellows. You could see from afar
the white of their eyeballs glistening. They shouted,
sang; their bodies streamed with perspiration; they had
faces like grotesque masks—these chaps; but they had
bone, muscles, a wild vitality, an intense energy of
movement, that was as natural and true as the surf
along their coast. They wanted no excuse for being
there. They were a great comfort to look at. For a
time I would feel I belonged still to a world of straightforward facts; but the feeling would not last long.

Something would turn up to scare it away. Once, I remember, we came upon a man-of-war anchored off the coast. There wasn't even a shed there, and she was shelling the bush. It appears the French had one of their wars going on thereabouts. Her ensign dropped limp like a rag; the muzzles of the long six-inch guns stuck out all over the low hull; the greasy, slimy swell swung her up lazily and let her down, swaying her thin masts. In the empty immensity of earth, sky, and water, there she was, incomprehensible, firing into a continent. Pop, would go one of the six-inch guns; a small flame would dart and vanish, a little white smoke would disappear, a tiny projectile would give a feeble screech—and nothing happened. Nothing could happen. There was a touch of insanity in the proceeding, a sense of lugubrious drollery in the sight; and it was not dissipated by somebody on board assuring me earnestly there was a camp of natives—he called them enemies!—hidden out of sight somewhere.

"We gave her her letters (I heard the men in that lonely ship were dying of fever at the rate of three a day) and went on. We called at some more places with farcical names, where the merry dance of death and trade goes on in a still and earthy atmosphere as of an overheated catacomb; all along the formless coast bordered by dangerous surf, as if Nature herself had tried to ward off intruders; in and out of rivers, streams of death in life, whose banks were rotting into mud, whose waters, thickened into slime, invaded the contorted mangroves, that seemed to writhe at us in the extremity of an impotent despair. Nowhere did we stop long enough to get a particularized impression, but the general sense of vague and oppressive wonder grew upon me. It was like a weary pilgrimage amongst hints for nightmares.

"It was upward of thirty days before I saw the mouth of the big river. We anchored off the seat of the government. But my work would not begin till some two hundred miles farther on. So as soon as I could I made a start for a place thirty miles higher up.

"I had my passage on a little sea-going steamer. Her captain was a Swede, and knowing me for a seaman, invited me on the bridge. He was a young man, lean, fair, and morose, with lanky hair and a shuffling gait. As we left the miserable little wharf, he tossed his head contemptuously at the shore. 'Been living there?' he asked. I said, 'Yes.' 'Fine lot these government chaps—are they not?' he went on, speaking English with great precision and considerable bitterness. 'It is funny what some people will do for a few francs a month. I wonder what becomes of that kind when it goes up country?' I said to him I expected to see that soon. 'So-o-o!' he exclaimed. He shuffled athwart, keeping one eye ahead vigilantly. 'Don't be too sure,' he continued. 'The other day I took up a man who hanged himself on the road. He was a Swede, too.' 'Hanged himself! Why, in God's name?' I cried. He kept on looking out watchfully. 'Who knows? The sun too much for him, or the country perhaps.'

"At last we opened a reach. A rocky cliff appeared, mounds of turned-up earth by the shore, houses on a hill, others with iron roofs, amongst a waste of excavations, or hanging to the declivity. A continuous noise of the rapids above hovered over this scene of inhabited devastation. A lot of people, mostly black and naked, moved about like ants. A jetty projected into the

river. A blinding sunlight drowned all this at ti⌒
a sudden recrudescence of glare. 'There's your C
pany's station,' said the Swede, pointing to th⌒
wooden barrack-like structures on the rocky slope. 'I
will send your things up. Four boxes did you say? So.
Farewell.'

"I came upon a boiler wallowing in the grass, then
found a path leading up the hill. It turned aside for
the boulders, and also for an undersized railway-truck
lying there on its back with its wheels in the air. One
was off. The thing looked as dead as the carcass of
some animal. I came upon more pieces of decaying
machinery, a stack of rusty rails. To the left a clump of
trees made a shady spot, where dark things seemed to
stir feebly. I blinked, the path was steep. A horn tooted
to the right, and I saw the black people run. A heavy
and dull detonation shook the ground, a puff of smoke
came out of the cliff, and that was all. No change appeared on the face of the rock. They were building a
railway. The cliff was not in the way or anything; but
this objectless blasting was all the work going on.

"A slight clinking behind me made me turn my head.
Six black men advanced in a file, toiling up the path.
They walked erect and slow, balancing small baskets
full of earth on their heads, and the clink kept time
with their footsteps. Black rags were wound round
their loins and the short ends behind waggled to and
fro like tails. I could see every rib, the joints of their
limbs were like knots in a rope; each had an iron
collar on his neck, and all were connected together
with a chain whose bights swung between them,
rhythmically clinking. Another report from the cliff
made me think suddenly of that ship of war I had

seen firing into a continent. It was the same kind of ominous voice; but these men could by no stretch of imagination be called enemies. They were called criminals, and the outraged law, like the bursting shells, had come to them, an insoluble mystery from the sea. All their meagre breasts panted together, the violently dilated nostrils quivered, the eyes stared stonily up-hill. They passed me within six inches, without a glance, with that complete, deathlike indifference of unhappy savages. Behind this raw matter one of the reclaimed, the product of the new forces at work, strolled despondently, carrying a rifle by its middle. He had a uniform jacket with one button off, and seeing a white man on the path, hoisted his weapon to his shoulder with alacrity. This was simple prudence, white men being so much alike at a distance that he could not tell who I might be. He was speedily reassured, and with a large, white, rascally grin, and a glance at his charge, seemed to take me into partnership in his exalted trust. After all, I also was a part of the great cause of these high and just proceedings.

"Instead of going up, I turned and descended to the left. My idea was to let that chain-gang get out of sight before I climbed the hill. You know I am not particularly tender; I've had to strike and to fend off. I've had to resist and to attack sometimes—that's only one way of resisting—without counting the exact cost, according to the demands of such sort of life as I had blundered into. I've seen the devil of violence, and the devil of greed, and the devil of hot desire; but, by all the stars! these were strong, lusty, red-eyed devils, that swayed and drove men—men, I tell you. But as I stood on this hillside, I foresaw that in the blinding sunshine of that land I would become acquainted with a flabby, pretending, weak-eyed devil of a rapacious and pitiless folly. How insidious he could be, too, I was only to find out several months later and a thousand miles farther. For a moment I stood appalled, as though by a warning. Finally I descended the hill, obliquely, towards the trees I had seen.

"I avoided a vast artificial hole somebody had been digging on the slope, the purpose of which I found it impossible to divine. It wasn't a quarry or a sandpit, anyhow. It was just a hole. It might have been connected with the philanthropic desire of giving the criminals something to do. I don't know. Then I nearly fell into a very narrow ravine, almost no more than a scar in the hillside. I discovered that a lot of imported drainage-pipes for the settlement had been tumbled in there. There wasn't one that was not broken. It was a wanton smash-up. At last I got under the trees. My purpose was to stroll into the shade for a moment; but no sooner within than it seemed to me I had stepped into the gloomy circle of some Inferno. The rapids were near, and an uninterrupted, uniform, headlong, rushing noise filled the mournful stillness of the grove, where not a breath stirred, not a leaf moved, with a mysterious sound—as though the tearing pace of the launched earth had suddenly become audible.

"Black shapes crouched, lay, sat between the trees leaning against the trunks, clinging to the earth, half coming out, half effaced within the dim light, in all the attitudes of pain, abandonment, and despair. Another mine on the cliff went off, followed by a slight shudder of the soil under my feet. The work was going on. The

work! And this was the place where some of the helpers
had withdrawn to die.

"They were dying slowly—it was very clear. They
were not enemies, they were not criminals, they were
nothing earthly now,—nothing but black shadows of
disease and starvation, lying confusedly in the greenish
gloom. Brought from all the recesses of the coast in all
the legality of time contracts, lost in uncongenial surroundings, fed on unfamiliar food, they sickened, became inefficient, and were then allowed to crawl away
and rest. These moribund shapes were free as air—and
nearly as thin. I began to distinguish the gleam of the
eyes under the trees. Then, glancing down, I saw a face
near my hand. The black bones reclined at full length
with one shoulder against the tree, and slowly the eyelids rose and the sunken eyes looked up at me,
enormous and vacant, a kind of blind, white flicker in
the depths of the orbs, which died out slowly. The man
seemed young—almost a boy—but you know with them
it's hard to tell. I found nothing else to do but to offer
him one of my good Swede's ship's biscuits I had in
my pocket. The fingers closed slowly on it and held—
there was no other movement and no other glance. He
had tied a bit of white worsted round his neck—Why?
angles Where did he get it? Was it a badge—an ornament—a
charm—a propitiatory act? Was there any idea at all
connected with it? It looked startling round his black
neck, this bit of white thread from beyond the seas.

"Near the same tree two more bundles of acute
angles sat with their legs drawn up. One, with his
chin propped on his knees, stared at nothing, in an
intolerable and appalling manner; his brother phantom
rested its forehead, as if overcome with a great weari-

ness; and all about others were scattered in every pose of contorted collapse, as in some picture of a massacre or a pestilence. While I stood horror-stricken, one of these creatures rose to his hands and knees, and went off on all-fours towards the river to drink. He lapped out of his hand, then sat up in the sunlight, crossing his shins in front of him, and after a time let his woolly head fall on his breastbone.

"I didn't want any more loitering in the shade, and I made haste towards the station. When near the buildings I met a white man, in such an unexpected elegance of get-up that in the first moment I took him for a sort of vision. I saw a high starched collar, white cuffs, a light alpaca jacket, snowy trousers, a clean necktie, and varnished boots. No hat. Hair parted, brushed, oiled, under a green-lined parasol held in a big white hand. He was amazing, and had a penholder behind his ear.

"I shook hands with this miracle, and I learned he was the Company's chief accountant, and that all the bookkeeping was done at this station. He had come out for a moment, he said, 'to get a breath of fresh air.' The expression sounded wonderfully odd, with its suggestion of sedentary desk-life. I wouldn't have mentioned the fellow to you at all, only it was from his lips that I first heard the name of the man who is so indissolubly connected with the memories of that time. Moreover, I respected the fellow. Yes; I respected his collars, his vast cuffs, his brushed hair. His appearance was certainly that of a hair-dresser's dummy; but in the great demoralization of the land he kept up his appearance. That's backbone. His starched collars and got-up shirt-fronts were achievements of character. He had been out nearly three years; and, later, I could not help asking him how he managed to sport such linen. He had just the faintest blush, and said modestly, 'I've been teaching one of the native women about the station. It was difficult. She had a distaste for the work.' Thus this man had verily accomplished something. And he was devoted to his books, which were in apple-pie order.

"Everything else in the station was in a muddle,— heads, things, buildings. Strings of dusty niggers with splay feet arrived and departed; a stream of manufactured goods, rubbishy cottons, beads, and brass-wire set into the depths of darkness, and in return came a precious trickle of ivory.

"I had to wait in the station for ten days—an eternity. I lived in a hut in the yard, but to be out of the chaos I would sometimes get into the accountant's office. It was built of horizontal planks, and so badly put together that, as he bent over his high desk, he was barred from neck to heels with narrow strips of sunlight. There was no need to open the big shutter to see. It was hot there, too; big flies buzzed fiendishly, and did not sting, but stabbed. I sat generally on the floor, while, of faultless appearance (and even slightly scented), perching on a high stool, he wrote, he wrote. Sometimes he stood up for exercise. When a truckle-bed with a sick man (some invalid agent from up-country) was put in there, he exhibited a gentle annoyance. 'The groans of this sick person,' he said, 'distract my attention. And without that it is extremely difficult to guard against clerical errors in this climate.'

"One day he remarked, without lifting his head, 'In the interior you will no doubt meet Mr. Kurtz.' On my

asking who Mr. Kurtz was, he said he was a first-class
agent; and seeing my disappointment at this information, he added slowly, laying down his pen. 'He is a
very remarkable person.' Further questions elicited
from him that Mr. Kurtz was at present in charge of a
trading post, a very important one, in the true ivory-
country, at 'the very bottom of there. Sends in as much
ivory as all the others put together . . .' He began to
write again. The sick man was too ill to groan. The
flies buzzed in a great peace.

"Suddenly there was a growing murmur of voices
and a great tramping of feet. A caravan had come in. A
violent babble of uncouth sounds burst out on the other
side of the planks. All the carriers were speaking together, and in the midst of the uproar the lamentable
voice of the chief agent was heard 'giving it up' tear-
fully for the twentieth time that day. . . . He rose
slowly. 'What a frightful row,' he said. He crossed the
room gently to look at the sick man, and returning,
said to me, 'He does not hear.' 'What! Dead?' I asked,
startled. 'No, not yet,' he answered, with great com-
posure. Then, alluding with a toss of the head to the
tumult in the station-yard, 'When one has got to make
correct entries, one comes to hate those savages—hate
them to the death.' He remained thoughtful for a moment. 'When you see Mr. Kurtz,' he went on, 'tell him
from me that everything here'—he glanced at the desk
—'is very satisfactory. I don't like to write to him—
with those messengers of ours you never know who
may get hold of your letter—at that Central Station.'
He stared at me for a moment with his mild, bulging
eyes. 'Oh, he will go far, very far,' he began again.
'He will be a somebody in the Administration before

long. They, above—the Council in Europe, you know —mean him to be.'

"He turned to his work. The noise outside had ceased, and presently in going out I stopped at the door. In the steady buzz of flies the homeward-bound agent was lying flushed and insensible; the other, bent over his books, was making correct entries of perfectly correct transactions; and fifty feet below the doorstep I could see the still tree-tops of the grove of death.

"Next day I left that station at last, with a caravan of sixty men, for a two-hundred-mile tramp.

"No use telling you much about that. Paths, paths, everywhere; a stamped-in network of paths spreading over the empty land, through long grass, through burnt grass, through thickets, down and up chilly ravines, up and down stony hills ablaze with heat; and a solitude, a solitude, nobody, not a hut. The population had cleared out a long time ago. Well, if a lot of mysterious niggers armed with all kinds of fearful weapons suddenly took to travelling on the road between Deal and Gravesend, catching the yokels right and left to carry heavy loads for them, I fancy every farm and cottage thereabouts would get empty very soon. Only here the dwellings were gone, too. Still I passed through several abandoned villages. There's something pathetically childish in the ruins of grass walls. Day after day, with the stamp and shuffle of sixty pair of bare feet behind me, each pair under a 60-lb. load. Camp, cook, sleep, strike camp, march. Now and then a carrier dead in harness, at rest in the long grass near the path, with an empty water-gourd and his long staff lying by his side. A great silence around and above. Perhaps on some quiet night the tremor of far-off drums, sinking, swelling, a tremor vast, faint; a sound weird, appealing, suggestive, and wild—and perhaps with as profound a meaning as the sound of bells in a Christian country. Once a white man in an unbuttoned uniform, camping on the path with an armed escort of lank Zanzibaris, very hospitable and festive—not to say drunk. Was looking after the upkeep of the road, he declared. Can't say I saw any road or any upkeep, unless the body of a middle-aged Negro, with a bullet-hole in the forehead, upon which I absolutely stumbled three miles farther on, may be considered as a permanent improvement. I had a white companion, too, not a bad chap, but rather too fleshy and with the exasperating habit of fainting on the hot hillsides, miles away from the least bit of shade and water. Annoying, you know, to hold your own coat like a parasol over a man's head while he is coming-to. I couldn't help asking him once what he meant by coming there at all. 'To make money, of course. What do you think?' he said, scornfully. Then he got fever, and had to be carried in a hammock slung under a pole. As he weighed sixteen stone I had no end of rows with the carriers. They jibbed, ran away, sneaked off with their loads in the night—quite a mutiny. So, one evening, I made a speech in English with gestures, not one of which was lost to the sixty pairs of eyes before me, and the next morning I started the hammock off in front all right. An hour afterwards I came upon the whole concern wrecked in a bush—man, hammock, groans, blankets, horrors. The heavy pole had skinned his poor nose. He was very anxious for me to kill somebody, but there wasn't the shadow of a carrier near. I remember the old doctor—'It would be interesting for science to watch the mental changes of in-

dividuals, on the spot.' I felt I was becoming scientifi-
cally interesting. However, all that is to no purpose. On
the fifteenth day I came in sight of the big river again,
and hobbled into the Central Station. It was on a back
water surrounded by scrub and forest, with a pretty
border of smelly mud on one side, and on the three
others enclosed by a crazy fence of rushes. A neglected
gap was all the gate it had, and the first glance at the
place was enough to let you see the flabby devil was
running that show. White men with long staves in their
hands appeared languidly from amongst the buildings,
strolling up to take a look at me, and then retired out
of sight somewhere. One of them, a stout, excitable
chap with black moustaches, informed me with great
volubility and many digressions, as soon as I told him
who I was, that my steamer was at the bottom of the
river. I was thunderstruck. What, how, why? Oh, it was
'all right.' The 'manager himself' was there. All quite
correct. 'Everybody had behaved splendidly! splendidly!'—'you must,' he said in agitation, 'go and see the
general manager at once. He is waiting!'

"I did not see the real significance of that wreck at
once. I fancy I see it now, but I am not sure—not at all.
Certainly the affair was too stupid—when I think of it—
to be altogether natural. Still . . . But at the moment it
presented itself simply as a confounded nuisance. The
steamer was sunk. They had started two days before in
a sudden hurry up the river with the manager on board,
in charge of some volunteer skipper, and before they
had been out three hours they tore the bottom out of
her on stones, and she sank near the south bank. I
asked myself what I was to do there, now my boat was
lost. As a matter of fact, I had plenty to do in fishing

my command out of the river. I had to set about it the
very next day. That, and the repairs when I brought
the pieces to the station, took some months.

"My first interview with the manager was curious.
He did not ask me to sit down after my twenty-mile
walk that morning. He was commonplace in complexion, in manners, and in voice. He was of middle size
and of ordinary build. His eyes, of the usual blue, were
perhaps remarkably cold, and he certainly could make
his glance fall on one as trenchant and heavy as an axe.
But even at these times the rest of his person seemed
to disclaim the intention. Otherwise there was only
an indefinable, faint expression of his lips, something
stealthy—a smile—not a smile—I remember it, but I
can't explain. It was unconscious, this smile was,
though just after he had said something it got intensi-
fied for an instant. It came at the end of his speeches
like a seal applied on the words to make the meaning
of the commonest phrase appear absolutely inscrutable.
He was a common trader, from his youth up employed
in these parts—nothing more. He was obeyed, yet he
inspired neither love nor fear, nor even respect. He inspired uneasiness. That was it! Uneasiness. Not a defi-
nite mistrust—just uneasiness—nothing more. You have
no idea how effective such a . . . a . . . faculty can be.
He had no genius for organizing, for initiative, or for
order even. That was evident in such things as the deplorable state of the station. He had no learning, and
no intelligence. His position had come to him—why?
Perhaps because he was never ill . . . He had served
three terms of three years out there . . . Because triumphant health in the general rout of constitutions is
a kind of power in itself. When he went home on leave

he rioted on a large scale—pompously. Jack ashore—
with a difference—in externals only. This one could
gather from his casual talk. He originated nothing, he
could keep the routine going—that's all. But he was
great. He was great by this little thing that it was impossible to tell what could control such a man. He
never gave that secret away. Perhaps there was nothing within him. Such a suspicion made one pause—for
out there there were no external checks. Once when
various tropical diseases had laid low almost every
'agent' in the station, he was heard to say, 'Men who
come out here should have no entrails.' He sealed the
utterance with that smile of his, as though it had been
a door opening into a darkness he had in his keeping.
You fancied you had seen things—but the seal was on.
When annoyed at meal-times by the constant quarrels
of the white men about precedence, he ordered an immense round table to be made, for which a special
house had to be built. This was the station's mess-room.
Where he sat was the first place—the rest were nowhere. One felt this to be his unalterable conviction.
He was neither civil nor uncivil. He was quiet. He allowed his 'boy'—an overfed young Negro from the
coast—to treat the white men, under his very eyes, with
provoking insolence.

"He began to speak as soon as he saw me. I had been
very long on the road. He could not wait. Had to start
without me. The up-river stations had to be relieved.
There had been so many delays already that he did not
know who was dead and who was alive, and how they
got on—and so on, and so on. He paid no attention to
my explanations, and, playing with a stick of sealing-
wax, repeated several times that the situation was 'very

grave, very grave.' There were rumours that a very important station was in jeopardy, and its chief, Mr. Kurtz, was ill. Hoped it was not true. Mr. Kurtz was . . . I felt weary and irritable. Hang Kurtz, I thought. I interrupted him by saying I had heard of Mr. Kurtz on the coast. 'Ah! So they talk of him down there,' he murmured to himself. Then he began again, assuring me Mr. Kurtz was the best agent he had, an exceptional man, of the greatest importance to the Company; therefore I could understand his anxiety. He was, he said, 'very, very uneasy.' Certainly he fidgeted on his chair a good deal, exclaimed, 'Ah, Mr. Kurtz!' broke the stick of sealing-wax and seemed dumbfounded by the accident. Next thing he wanted to know 'how long it would take to.' . . . I interrupted him again. Being hungry, you know, and kept on my feet too, I was getting savage. 'How can I tell?' I said. 'I haven't even seen the wreck yet—some months, no doubt.' All this talk seemed to me so futile. 'Some months,' he said. Well, let us say three months before we can make a start. Yes. That ought to do the affair.' I flung out of his hut (he lived all alone in a clay hut with a sort of verandah) muttering to myself my opinion of him. He was a chattering idiot. Afterwards I took it back when it was borne in upon me startlingly with what extreme nicety he had estimated the time requisite for the 'affair.'

"I went to work the next day, turning, so to speak, my back on that station. In that way only it seemed to me I could keep my hold on the redeeming facts of life. Still, one must look about sometimes; and then I saw this station, these men strolling aimlessly about in the sunshine of the yard. I asked myself sometimes what it all meant. They wandered here and there with their

absurd long staves in their hands, like a lot of faithless
pilgrims bewitched inside a rotten fence. The word
'ivory' rang in the air, was whispered, was sighed. You
would think they were praying to it. A taint of imbecile
rapacity blew through it all, like a whiff from some
corpse. By Jove! I've never seen anything so unreal in
my life. And outside, the silent wilderness surrounding
this cleared speck on the earth struck me as something
great and invincible, like evil or truth, waiting patiently for the passing away of this fantastic invasion.

"Oh, these months! Well, never mind. Various things
happened. One evening a grass shed full of calico, cotton prints, beads, and I don't know what else, burst
into a blaze so suddenly that you would have thought
the earth had opened to let an avenging fire consume
all that trash. I was smoking my pipe quietly by my
dismantled steamer, and saw them all cutting capers in
the light, with their arms lifted high, when the stout
man with moustaches came tearing down to the river,
a tin pail in his hand, assured me that everybody was
'behaving splendidly, splendidly,' dipped about a quart
of water and tore back again. I noticed there was a
hole in the bottom of his pail.

"I strolled up. There was no hurry. You see the thing
had gone off like a box of matches. It had been hopeless from the very first. The flame had leaped high,
driven everybody back, lighted up everything—and
collapsed. The shed was already a heap of embers
glowing fiercely. A nigger was being beaten near by.
They said he had caused the fire in some way; be that
as it may, he was screeching most horribly. I saw him,
later, for several days, sitting in a bit of shade looking
very sick and trying to recover himself: afterwards he

arose and went out—and the wilderness without a
sound took him into its bosom again. As I approached
the glow from the dark I found myself at the back of
two men, talking. I heard the name of Kurtz pronounced, then the words, 'take advantage of this unfor-
tunate accident.' One of the men was the manager. I
wished him a good evening. 'Did you ever see anything
like it—eh? it is incredible,' he said, and walked off.
The other man remained. He was a first-class agent,
young, gentlemanly, a bit reserved, with a forked little
beard and a hooked nose. He was stand-offish with the
other agents, and they on their side said he was the
manager's spy upon them. As to me, I had hardly ever
spoken to him before. We got into talk, and by and by
we strolled away from the hissing ruins. Then he asked
me to his room, which was in the main building of the
station. He struck a match, and I perceived that this
young aristocrat had not only a silver-mounted dress-
ing-case but also a whole candle all to himself. Just at
that time the manager was the only man supposed to
have any right to candles. Native mats covered the clay
walls; a collection of spears, assegais, shields, knives
was hung up in trophies. The business intrusted to this
fellow was the making of bricks—so I had been informed; but there wasn't a fragment of a brick anywhere in the station, and he had been there more than
a year—waiting. It seems he could not make bricks
without something, I don't know what—straw maybe.
Anyways, it could not be found there, and as it was not
likely to be sent from Europe, it did not appear clear to
me what he was waiting for. An act of special creation
perhaps. However, they were all waiting—all the sixteen or twenty pilgrims of them—for something; and

upon my word it did not seem an uncongenial occupation, from the way they took it, though the only thing that ever came to them was disease—as far as I could see. They beguiled the time by backbiting and intriguing against each other in a foolish kind of way. There was an air of plotting about that station, but nothing came of it, of course. It was as unreal as everything else—as the philanthropic pretence of the whole concern, as their talk, as their government, as their show of work. The only real feeling was a desire to get appointed to a trading-post where ivory was to be had, so that they could earn percentages. They intrigued and slandered and hated each other only on that account,—but as to effectually lifting a little finger—oh, no. By heavens! there is something after all in the world allowing one man to steal a horse while another must not look at a halter. Steal a horse straight out. Very well. He has done it. Perhaps he can ride. But there is way of looking at a halter that would provoke the most charitable of saints into a kick.

I had no idea why he wanted to be sociable, but as we chatted in there it suddenly occurred to me the fellow was trying to get at something—in fact, pumping me. He alluded constantly to Europe, to the people I was supposed to know there—putting leading questions as to my acquaintances in the sepulchral city, and so on. His little eyes glittered like mica discs—with curiosity—though he tried to keep up a bit of superciliousness. At first I was astonished, but very soon I became awfully curious to see what he would find out from me. I couldn't possibly imagine what I had in me to make it worth his while. It was very pretty to see how he baffled himself, for in truth my body was full only of chills, and my head had nothing in it but that wretched steamboat business. It was evident he took me for a perfectly shameless prevaricator. At last he got angry, and, to conceal a movement of furious annoyance, he yawned. I rose. Then I noticed a small sketch in oils, on a panel, representing a woman, draped and blind-folded, carrying a lighted torch. The background was sombre—almost black. The movement of the woman was stately, and the effect of the torch-light on the face was sinister.

"It arrested me, and he stood by civilly, holding an empty half-pint champagne bottle (medical comforts) with the candle stuck in it. To my question he said Mr. Kurtz had painted this—in this very station more than a year ago—while waiting for means to go to his trad-ing-post. 'Tell me, pray,' said I, 'who is this Mr. Kurtz?'

" 'The chief of the Inner Station,' he answered in a short tone, looking away. 'Much obliged,' I said, laugh-ing. 'And you are the brick-maker of the Central Sta-tion. Everyone knows that.' He was silent for a while. 'He is a prodigy,' he said at last. 'He is an emissary of pity, and science, and progress, and devil knows what else. We want,' he began to declaim suddenly, 'for the guidance of the cause intrusted to us by Europe, so to speak, higher intelligence, wide sympathies, a single-ness of purpose.' 'Who says that?' I asked. 'Lots of them,' he replied. 'Some even write that; and so *he* comes here, a special being, as you ought to know.' 'Why ought I to know?' I interrupted, really surprised. He paid no attention. 'Yes. To-day he is chief of the best station, next year he will be assistant-manager, two years more and . . . but I daresay you know what he will be in two years' time. You are of the new gang

—the gang of virtue. The same people who sent him specially also recommended you. Oh, don't say no. I've my own eyes to trust.' Light dawned upon me. My dear aunt's influential acquaintances were producing an unexpected effect upon that young man. I nearly burst into a laugh. 'Do you read the Company's confidential correspondence?' I asked. He hadn't a word to say. It was great fun. 'When Mr. Kurtz,' I continued, severely, 'is General Manager, you won't have the opportunity.'

"He blew the candle out suddenly, and we went outside. The moon had risen. Black figures strolled about listlessly, pouring water on the glow, whence proceeded a sound of hissing; steam ascended in the moonlight, the beaten nigger groaned somewhere. 'What a row the brute makes!' said the indefatigable man with the moustaches, appearing near us. 'Serve him right. Transgression—punishment—bang! Pitiless, pitiless. That's the only way. This will prevent all conflagrations for the future. I was just telling the manager . . .' He noticed my companion, and became crestfallen all at once. 'Not in bed yet,' he said, with a kind of servile heartiness; 'it's so natural. Ha! Danger—agitation.' He vanished. I went on to the river-side, and the other followed me. I heard a scathing murmur at my ear, 'Heap of muffs—got to.' The pilgrims could be seen in knots gesticulating, discussing. Several had still their staves in their hands. I verily believe they took these sticks to bed with them. Beyond the fence the forest stood up spectrally in the moonlight, and through the dim stir, through the faint sounds of that lamentable courtyard, the silence of the land went home to one's very heart—its mystery, its greatness, the amazing reality of its concealed life. The hurt nigger moaned

feebly somewhere near by, and then fetched a deep
sigh that made me mend my pace away from there. I
felt a hand introducing itself under my arm. 'My dear
sir,' said the fellow, 'I don't want to be misunderstood,
and especially by you, who will see Mr. Kurtz long before I can have that pleasure. I wouldn't like him to get
a false idea of my disposition. . . .'

"I let him run on, this papier-mâché Mephistopheles,
and it seemed to me that if I tried I could poke my
forefinger through him, and would find nothing inside
but a little loose dirt, maybe. He, don't you see, had
been planning to be assistant-manager by and by under the present man, and I could see that the coming of
that Kurtz had upset them both not a little. He talked
precipitately, and I did not try to stop him. I had my
shoulders against the wreck of my steamer, hauled up
on the slope like a carcass of some big river animal.
The smell of mud, of primeval mud, by Jove! was in
my nostrils, the high stillness of primeval forest was before my eyes; there were shiny patches on the black
creek. The moon had spread over everything a thin
layer of silver—over the rank grass, over the mud, upon
the wall of matted vegetation standing higher than the
wall of a temple, over the great river I could see
through a sombre gap glittering, glittering, as it flowed
broadly by without a murmur. All this was great, ex-
pectant, mute, while the man jabbered about himself.
I wondered whether the stillness on the face of the immensity looking at us two were meant as an appeal or
as a menace. What were we who had strayed in here?
Could we handle that dumb thing, or would it handle
us? I felt how big, how confoundedly big, was that
thing that couldn't talk, and perhaps was deaf as well.

What was in there? I could see a little ivory coming out from there, and I had heard Mr. Kurtz was in there. I had heard enough about it, too—God knows! Yet somehow it didn't bring any image with it—no more than if I had been told an angel or a fiend was in there. I believed it in the same way one of you might believe there are inhabitants in the planet Mars. I knew once a Scotch sailmaker who was certain, dead sure, there were people in Mars. If you asked him for some idea how they looked and behaved, he would get shy and mutter something about 'walking on all-fours.' If you as much as smiled, he would—though a man of sixty—offer to fight you. I would not have gone so far as to fight for Kurtz, but I went for him near enough to a lie. You know I hate, detest, and can't bear a lie, not because I am straighter than the rest of us, but simply because it appalls me. There is a taint of death, a flavour of mortality in lies—which is exactly what I hate and detest in the world—what I want to forget. It makes me miserable and sick, like biting something rotten would do. Temperament, I suppose. Well, I went near enough to it by letting the young fool there believe anything he liked to imagine as to my influence in Europe. I became in an instant as much of a pretence as the rest of the bewitched pilgrims. This simply because I had a notion it somehow would be of help to that Kurtz whom at the time I did not see—you understand. He was just a word for me. I did not see the man in the name any more than you do. Do you see him? Do you see the story? Do you see anything? It seems to me I am trying to tell you a dream—making a vain attempt, because no relation of a dream can convey the dream-sensation, that commingling of absurdity, surprise, and

bewilderment in a tremor of struggling revolt, that notion of being captured by the incredible which is of
the very essence of dreams...."

He was silent for a while.

"... No, it is impossible; it is impossible to convey
the life-sensation of any given epoch of one's existence
—that which makes its truth, its meaning—its subtle and
penetrating essence. It is impossible. We live, as we
dream—alone...."

He paused again as if reflecting, then added—

"Of course in this you fellows see more than I could
then. You see me, whom you know...."

It had become so pitch dark that we listeners could
hardly see one another. For a long time already he, sitting apart, had been no more to us than a voice. There
was not a word from anybody. The others might have
been asleep, but I was awake. I listened, I listened on
the watch for the sentence, for the word, that would
give me the clue to the faint uneasiness inspired by this
narrative that seemed to shape itself without human
lips in the heavy night-air of the river.

"... Yes—I let him run on," Marlow began again,
"and think what he pleased about the powers that were
behind me. I did! And there was nothing behind me!
There was nothing but that wretched, old, mangled
steamboat I was leaning against, while he talked fluent-
ly about 'the necessity for every man to get on.' 'And
when one comes out here, you conceive, it is not to
gaze at the moon.' Mr. Kurtz was a 'universal genius,'
but even a genius would find it easier to work with
'adequate tools—intelligent men.' He did not make
bricks—why, there was a physical impossibility in the
way—as I was well aware; and if he did secretarial

work for the manager, it was because 'no sensible man rejects wantonly the confidence of his superiors.' Did I see it? I saw it. What more did I want? What I really wanted was rivets, by heaven! Rivets. To get on with the work—to stop the hole. Rivets I wanted. There were cases of them down at the coast—cases—piled up—burst —split! You kicked a loose rivet at every second step in that station yard on the hillside. Rivets had rolled into the grove of death. You could fill your pockets with rivets for the trouble of stooping down—and there wasn't one rivet to be found where it was wanted. We had plates that would do, but nothing to fasten them with. And every week the messenger, a lone Negro, letter-bag on shoulder and staff in hand, left our station for the coast. And several times a week a coast caravan came in with trade goods—ghastly glazed calico that made you shudder only to look at it, glass beads value about a penny a quart, confounded spotted cotton handkerchiefs. And no rivets. Three carriers could have brought all that was wanted to set that steamboat afloat.

"He was becoming confidential now, but I fancy my unresponsive attitude must have exasperated him at last, for he judged it necessary to inform me he feared neither God nor devil, let alone any mere man. I said I could see that very well, but what I wanted was a certain quantity of rivets—and rivets were what really Mr. Kurtz wanted, if he had only known it. Now letters went to the coast every week. . . . 'My dear sir,' he cried, 'I write from dictation.' I demanded rivets. There was a way—for an intelligent man. He changed his manner; became very cold, and suddenly began to talk about a hippopotamus; wondered whether sleeping on board the steamer (I stuck to my salvage night and day) I wasn't disturbed. There was an old hippo that had the bad habit of getting out on the bank and roaming at night over the station grounds. The pilgrims used to turn out in a body and empty every rifle they could lay hands on at him. Some even had sat up o' nights for him. All this energy was wasted, though. 'That animal has a charmed life,' he said; 'but you can say this only of brutes in this country. No man—you apprehend me?—no man here bears a charmed life.' He stood there for a moment in the moonlight with his delicate hooked nose set a little askew, and his mica eyes glittering without a wink, then, with a curt Goodnight, he strode off. I could see he was disturbed and considerably puzzled, which made me feel more hopeful than I had been for days. It was a great comfort to turn from that chap to my influential friend, the battered, twisted, ruined, tin-pot steamboat. I clambered on board. She rang under my feet like an empty Huntley & Palmer biscuit-tin kicked along a gutter; she was nothing so solid in make, and rather less pretty in shape, but I had expended enough hard work on her to make me love her. No influential friend would have served me better. She had given me a chance to come out a bit—to find out what I could do. No, I don't like work. I had rather laze about and think of all the fine things that can be done. I don't like work—no man does —but I like what is in the work,—the chance to find yourself. Your own reality—for yourself, not for others —what no other man can ever know. They can only see the mere show, and never can tell what it really means.

"I was not surprised to see somebody sitting aft, on the deck, with his legs dangling over the mud. You see

I rather chummed with the few mechanics there were in that station, whom the other pilgrims naturally despised—on account of their imperfect manners, I suppose. This was the foreman—a boiler-maker by trade—a good worker. He was a lank, bony, yellow-faced man, with big intense eyes. His aspect was worried, and his head was as bald as the palm of my hand; but his hair in falling seemed to have stuck to his chin, and had prospered in the new locality, for his beard hung down to his waist. He was a widower with six young children (he had left them in charge of a sister of his to come out there), and the passion of his life was pigeon-flying. He was an enthusiast and a connoisseur. He would rave about pigeons. After work hours he used sometimes to come over from his hut for a talk about his children and his pigeons; at work, when he had to crawl in the mud under the bottom of the steamboat, he would tie up that beard of his in a kind of white serviette he brought for the purpose. It had loops to go over his ears. In the evening he could be seen squatted on the bank rinsing that wrapper in the creek with great care, then spreading it solemnly on a bush to dry.

"I slapped him on the back and shouted, 'We shall have rivets!' He scrambled to his feet exclaiming, 'No! Rivets!' as though he couldn't believe his ears. Then in a low voice, 'You . . . eh?' I don't know why we behaved like lunatics. I put my finger to the side of my nose and nodded mysteriously. 'Good for you,' he cried, snapped his fingers above his head, lifting one foot. I tried a jig. We capered on the iron deck. A frightful clatter came out of that hulk, and the virgin forest on the other bank of the creek sent it back in a thundering roll upon the sleeping station. It must have made some of the pilgrims sit up in their hovels. A dark figure obscured the lighted doorway of the manager's hut, vanished, then, a second or so after, the doorway itself vanished, too. We stopped, and the silence driven away by the stamping of our feet flowed back again from the recesses of the land. The great wall of vegetation, an exuberant and entangled mass of trunks, branches, leaves, boughs, festoons, motionless in the moonlight, was like a rioting invasion of soundless life, a rolling wave of plants, piled up, crested, ready to topple over the creek, to sweep every little man of us out of his little existence. And it moved not. A deadened burst of mighty splashes and snorts reached us from afar, as though an ichthyosaurus had been taking a bath of glitter in the great river. 'After all,' said the boiler-maker in a reasonable tone, 'why shouldn't we get the rivets?' Why not, indeed! I did not know of any reason why we shouldn't. 'They'll come in three weeks,' I said, confidently.

"But they didn't. Instead of rivets there came an invasion, an infliction, a visitation. It came in sections during the next three weeks, each section headed by a donkey carrying a white man in new clothes and tan shoes, bowing from that elevation right and left to the impressed pilgrims. A quarrelsome band of footsore sulky niggers trod on the heels of the donkey; a lot of tents, camp-stools, tin boxes, white cases, brown bales would be shot down in the courtyard, and the air of mystery would deepen a little over the muddle of the station. Five such instalments came, with their absurd air of disorderly flight with the loot of innumerable outfit shops and provision stores, that, one would think, they were lugging, after a raid, into the wilderness for equitable division. It was an inextricable mess of things decent in themselves but that human folly made look like the spoils of thieving.

"This devoted band called itself the Eldorado Exploring Expedition, and I believe they were sworn to secrecy. Their talk, however, was the talk of sordid buccaneers: it was reckless without hardihood, greedy without audacity, and cruel without courage; there was not an atom of foresight or of serious intention in the whole batch of them, and they did not seem aware these things are wanted for the work of the world. To tear treasure out of the bowels of the land was their desire, with no more moral purpose at the back of it than there is in burglars breaking into a safe. Who paid the expenses of the noble enterprise I don't know; but the uncle of our manager was leader of that lot.

"In exterior he resembled a butcher in a poor neighbourhood, and his eyes had a look of sleepy cunning. He carried his fat paunch with ostentation on his short legs, and during the time his gang infested the station spoke to no one but his nephew. You could see these two roaming about all day long with their heads close together in an everlasting confab.

"I had given up worrying myself about the rivets. One's capacity for that kind of folly is more limited than you would suppose. I said Hang!—and let things slide. I had plenty of time for meditation, and now and then I would give some thought to Kurtz. I wasn't very interested in him. No. Still, I was curious to see whether this man, who had come out equipped with moral ideas of some sort, would climb to the top after all and how he would set about his work when there."

◇◇◇◇◇◇◇◇◇◇◇◇◇◇

CHAPTER

2

◇◇◇◇◇◇◇◇◇◇◇◇◇◇

"One evening as I was lying flat on the deck of my steamboat, I heard voices approaching—and there were the nephew and the uncle strolling along the bank. I laid my head on my arm again, and had nearly lost myself in a doze, when somebody said in my ear, as it were: 'I am as harmless as a little child, but I don't like to be dictated to. Am I the manager—or am I not? I was ordered to send him there. It's incredible.' . . . I became aware that the two were standing on the shore alongside the forepart of the steamboat, just below my head. I did not move; it did not occur to me to move: I was sleepy. 'It *is* unpleasant,' grunted the uncle. 'He has asked the Administration to be sent there,' said the other, 'with the idea of showing what he could do; and I was instructed accordingly. Look

47

.t the influence that man must have. Is it not frightful?' They both agreed it was frightful, then made several bizarre remarks: 'Make rain and fine weather— one man—the Council—by the nose'—bits of absurd sentences that got the better of my drowsiness, so that I had pretty near the whole of my wits about me when the uncle said, 'The climate may do away with this difficulty for you. Is he alone there?' 'Yes,' answered the manager; 'he sent his assistant down the river with a note to me in these terms: "Clear this poor devil out of the country, and don't bother sending more of that sort. I had rather be alone than have the kind of men you can dispose of with me." It was more than a year ago. Can you imagine such impudence!' 'Anything since then?' asked the other, hoarsely. 'Ivory,' jerked the nephew; 'lots of it—prime sort—lots—most annoying, from him.' 'And with that?' questioned the heavy rumble. 'Invoice,' was the reply fired out, so to speak. Then silence. They had been talking about Kurtz.

"I was broad awake by this time, but, lying perfectly at ease, remained still, having no inducement to change my position. 'How did that ivory come all this way?' growled the elder man, who seemed very vexed. The other explained that it had come with a fleet of canoes in charge of an English half-caste clerk Kurtz had with him; that Kurtz had apparently intended to return himself, the station being by that time bare of goods and stores, but after coming three hundred miles, had suddenly decided to go back, which he started to do alone in a small dugout with four paddlers, leaving the half-caste to continue down the river with the ivory. The two fellows there seemed astounded at anybody attempting such a thing. They were at a loss for an adequate motive. As to me, I seemed to see Kurtz for the first time. It was a distinct glimpse: the dugout, four paddling savages, and the lone white man turning his back suddenly on the headquarters, on relief, on thoughts of home—perhaps; setting his face towards the depths of the wilderness, towards his empty and desolate station. I did not know the motive. Perhaps he was just simply a fine fellow who stuck to his work for its own sake. His name, you understand, had not been pronounced once. He was 'that man.' The half-caste, who, as far as I could see, had conducted a difficult trip with great prudence and pluck, was invariably alluded to as 'that scoundrel.' The 'scoundrel' had reported that the 'man' had been very ill—had recovered imperfectly. . . . The two below me moved away then a few paces, and strolled back and forth at some little distance. I heard: 'Military post—doctor—two hundred miles—quite alone now—unavoidable delays—nine months—no news—strange rumours.' They approached again, just as the manager was saying, 'No one, as far as I know, unless a species of wandering trader—a pestilential fellow, snapping ivory from the natives.' Who was it they were talking about now? I gathered in snatches that this was some man supposed to be in Kurtz's district, and of whom the manager did not approve. 'We will not be free from unfair competition till one of these fellows is hanged for an example,' he said. 'Certainly,' grunted the other; 'get him hanged! Why not? Anything—anything can be done in this country. That's what I say; nobody here, you understand, *here*, can endanger your position. And why? You stand the climate—you outlast them all. The danger is in Europe; but there before I left I took care to

——' They moved off and whispered, then their voices rose again. 'The extraordinary series of delays is not my fault. I did my best.' The fat man sighed. 'Very sad.' 'And the pestiferous absurdity of his talk,' continued the other; 'he bothered me enough when he was here. "Each station should be like a beacon on the road towards better things, a centre for trade of course, but also for humanizing, improving, instructing." Conceive you—that ass! And he wants to be manager! No, it's ——' Here he got choked by excessive indignation, and I lifted my head the least bit. I was surprised to see how near they were—right under me. I could have spat upon their hats. They were looking on the ground, absorbed in thought. The manager was switching his leg with a slender twig: his sagacious relative lifted his head. 'You have been well since you came out this time?' he asked. The other gave a start. 'Who? I? Oh! Like a charm—like a charm. But the rest—oh, my goodness! All sick. They die so quick, too, that I haven't the time to send them out of the country—it's incredible!' 'H'm. Just so,' grunted the uncle. 'Ah! my boy, trust to this—I say, trust to this.' I saw him extend his short flipper of an arm for a gesture that took in the forest, the creek, the mud, the river,—seemed to beckon with a dishonouring flourish before the sunlit face of the land a treacherous appeal to the lurking death, to the hidden evil, to the profound darkness of its heart. It was so startling that I leaped to my feet and looked back at the edge of the forest, as though I had expected an answer of some sort to that black display of confidence. You know the foolish notions that come to one sometimes. The high stillness confronted these two figures with its ominous patience, waiting for the pass-ing away of a fantastic invasion.

"They swore aloud together—out of sheer fright, I be-lieve—then pretending not to know anything of my existence, turned back to the station. The sun was low; and leaning forward side by side, they seemed to be tugging painfully uphill their two ridiculous shadows of unequal length, that trailed behind them slowly over the tall grass without bending a single blade.

"In a few days the Eldorado Expedition went into the patient wilderness, that closed upon it as the sea closes over a diver. Long afterwards the news came that all the donkeys were dead. I know nothing as to the fate of the less valuable animals. They, no doubt, like the rest of us, found what they deserved. I did not inquire. I was then rather excited at the prospect of meeting Kurtz very soon. When I say very soon I mean it comparatively. It was just two months from the day we left the creek when we came to the bank below Kurtz's station.

"Going up that river was like travelling back to the earliest beginnings of the world, when vegetation rioted on the earth and the big trees were kings. An empty stream, a great silence, an impenetrable forest. The air was warm, thick, heavy, sluggish. There was no joy in the brilliance of sunshine. The long stretches of the waterway ran on, deserted, into the gloom of over-shadowed distances. On silvery sandbanks hippos and alligators sunned themselves side by side. The broad-ening water flowed through a mob of wooden islands; you lost your way on that river as you would in a des-ert, and butted all day long against shoals, trying to find the channel, till you thought yourself bewitched and cut off for ever from everything you had known once—somewhere—far away—in another existence perhaps. There were moments when one's past came back to one, as it will sometimes when you have not a moment to spare to yourself; but it came in the shape of an unrestful and noisy dream, remembered with wonder amongst the overwhelming realities of this strange world of plants, and water, and silence. And this stillness of life did not in the least resemble a peace. It was the stillness of an implacable force brooding over an inscrutable intention. It looked at you with a vengeful aspect. I got used to it afterwards; I did not see it any more; I had no time. I had to keep guessing at the channel; I had to discern, mostly by inspiration, the signs of hidden banks; I watched for sunken stones; I was learning to clap my teeth smartly before my heart flew out, when I shaved by a fluke some infernal sly old snag that would have ripped the life out of the tin-pot steamboat and drowned all the pilgrims; I had to keep a look-out for the signs of dead wood we could cut up in the night for next day's steaming. When you have to attend to things of that sort, to the mere incidents of the surface, the reality—the reality, I tell you—fades. The inner truth is hidden—luckily, luckily. But I felt it all the same; I felt often its mysterious stillness watching me at my monkey tricks, just as it watches you fellows performing on your respective tight-ropes for—what is it? half-a-crown a tumble——"

"Try to be civil, Marlow," growled a voice, and I knew there was at least one listener awake besides myself.

"I beg your pardon. I forgot the heartache which makes up the rest of the price. And indeed what does the price matter, if the trick be well done? You do your tricks very well. And I didn't do badly either, since I managed not to sink that steamboat on my first trip. It's a wonder to me yet. Imagine a blindfolded man set to drive a van over a bad road. I sweated and shivered over that business considerably, I can tell you. After all, for a seaman, to scrape the bottom of the thing that's supposed to float all the time under his care is the unpardonable sin. No one may know of it, but you never forget the thump—eh? A blow on the very heart. You remember it, you dream of it, you wake up at night and think of it—years after—and go hot and cold all over. I don't pretend to say that steamboat floated all the time. More than once she had to wade for a bit, with twenty cannibals splashing around and pushing. We had enlisted some of these chaps on the way for a crew. Fine fellows—cannibals—in their place. They were men one could work with, and I am grateful to them. And, after all, they did not eat each other before my face: they had brought along a provision of hippo-meat which went rotten, and made the mystery of the wilderness stink in my nostrils. Phoo! I can sniff it now. I had the manager on board and three or four pilgrims with their staves—all complete. Sometimes we came upon a station close by the bank, clinging to the skirts of the unknown, and the white men rushing out of a tumble-down hovel, with great gestures of joy and surprise and welcome, seemed very strange—had the appearance of being held there captive by a spell. The word ivory would ring in the air for a while—and on we went again into the silence, along empty reaches, round the still bends, between the high walls of our winding way, reverberating in hollow claps the ponderous beat of the stern-wheel. Trees, trees, millions of trees, massive, immense, running up high; and at their foot, hugging the bank against the stream, crept the little begrimed steamboat, like a sluggish beetle crawling on the floor of a lofty portico. It made you feel very small, very lost, and yet it was not altogether depressing, that feeling. After all, if you were small, the grimy beetle crawled on—which was just what you wanted it to do. Where the pilgrims imagined it crawled to I don't know. To some place where they expected to get something, I bet! For me it crawled towards Kurtz—exclusively; but when the steam-pipes started leaking we crawled very slow. The reaches opened before us and closed behind, as if the forest had stepped leisurely across the water to bar the way for our return. We penetrated deeper and deeper into the heart of darkness. It was very quiet there. At night sometimes the roll of drums behind the curtain of trees would run up the river and remain sustained faintly, as if hovering in the air high over our heads, till the first break of day. Whether it meant war, peace, or prayer we could not tell. The dawns were heralded by the descent of a chill stillness; the wood-cutters slept, their fires burned low; the snapping of a twig would make you start. We were wanderers on a prehistoric earth, on an earth that wore the aspect of an unknown planet. We could have fancied ourselves the first of men taking possession of an accursed inheritance, to be subdued at the cost of profound anguish and of excessive toil. But suddenly, as we struggled round a bend, there would be a glimpse of rush walls, of peaked grass-roofs, a burst of yells, a whirl of black limbs, a mass of hands clapping, of feet stamping, of bodies swaying, of eyes rolling, under the droop of heavy and motionless foliage. The steamer toiled along slowly on the edge of a black and incomprehensible frenzy. The prehistoric man was cursing us, praying to us, welcoming us—who could tell? We were cut off from the comprehension of our surroundings; we glided past like phantoms, wondering and secretly appalled, as sane men would be before an enthusiastic outbreak in a madhouse. We could not understand because we were too far and could not remember, because we were travelling in the night of first ages, of those ages that are gone, leaving hardly a sign—and no memories.

"The earth seemed unearthly. We are accustomed to look upon the shackled form of a conquered monster, but there—there you could look at a thing monstrous and free. It was unearthly, and the men were—— No, they were not inhuman. Well, you know, that was the worst of it—this suspicion of their not being inhuman. It would come slowly to one. They howled and leaped, and spun, and made horrid faces; but what thrilled you was just the thought of their humanity—like yours—the thought of your remote kinship with this wild and passionate uproar. Ugly. Yes, it was ugly enough; but if you were man enough you would admit to yourself that there was in you just the faintest trace of a response to the terrible frankness of that noise, a dim suspicion of there being a meaning in it which you—you so remote from the night of first ages—could comprehend. And why not? The mind of man is capable of anything—because everything is in it, all the past as well as all the future. What was there after all? Joy, fear, sorrow, devotion, valour, rage—who can tell?—but truth—truth stripped of its cloak of time. Let the fool gape and shudder—the man knows, and can look on without a wink. But he must at least be as much of a man as these on the shore. He must meet that truth with his own true stuff—with his own inborn strength. Principles won't do. Acquisitions, clothes, pretty rags—rags that would fly off at the first good shake. No; you want a deliberate belief. An appeal to me in this fiendish row—is there? Very well; I hear; I admit, but I have a voice, too, and for good or evil mine is the speech that cannot be silenced. Of course, a fool, what with sheer fright and fine sentiments, is always safe. Who's that grunting? You wonder I didn't go ashore for a howl and a dance? Well, no—I didn't. Fine sentiments, you say? Fine sentiments, be hanged! I had no time. I had to mess about with white-lead and strips of woollen blanket helping to put bandages on those leaky steam-pipes—I tell you. I had to watch the steering, and circumvent those snags, and get the tin-pot along by hook or by crook. There was surface-truth enough in these things to save a wiser man. And between whiles I had to look after the savage who was fireman. He was an improved specimen; he could fire up a vertical boiler. He was there below me, and, upon my word, to look at him was as edifying as seeing a dog in a parody of breeches and a feather hat, walking on his hind-legs. A few months of training had done for that really fine chap. He squinted at the steam-gauge and at the water-gauge with an evident effort of intrepidity—and he had filed teeth, too, the poor devil, and the wool of his pate shaved into queer patterns, and three ornamental scars on each of his cheeks. He ought to have been clapping his hands and stamping his feet on the bank, instead of which he was hard at work, a thrall to strange witch-craft, full of improving knowledge. He was useful be-cause he had been instructed; and what he knew was this—that should the water in that transparent thing disappear, the evil spirit inside the boiler would get angry through the greatness of his thirst, and take a terrible vengeance. So he sweated and fired up and watched the glass fearfully (with an impromptu charm, made of rags, tied to his arm, and a piece of polished bone, as big as a watch, struck flatways through his lower lip), while the wooded banks slipped past us slowly, the short noise was left behind, the intermin-able miles of silence—and we crept on, towards Kurtz. But the snags were thick, the water was treacherous and shallow, the boiler seemed indeed to have a sulky devil in it, and thus neither that fireman nor I had any time to peer into our creepy thoughts.

"Some fifty miles below the Inner Station we came upon a hut of reeds, an inclined and melancholy pole, with the unrecognizable tatters of what had been a flag of some sort flying from it, and a neatly stacked wood-pile. This was unexpected. We came to the bank, and on the stack of firewood found a flat piece of board with some faded pencil-writing on it. When deciphered it said: 'Wood for you. Hurry up. Approach cautiously.' There was a signature, but it was illegible—not Kurtz—a much longer word. 'Hurry up.' Where? Up the river? 'Approach cautiously.' We had not done so. But the warning could not have been meant for the place where it could be only found after approach. Something was wrong above. But what—and how much? That was the question. We commented adversely upon the imbecility of that telegraphic style. The bush around said nothing, and would not let us look very far, either. A torn curtain of red twill hung in the doorway of the hut, and flapped sadly in our faces. The dwelling was dismantled; but we could see a white man had lived there not very long ago. There remained a rude table—a plank on two posts; a heap of rubbish reposed in a dark corner, and by the door I picked up a book. It had lost its covers, and the pages had been thumbed into a state of extremely dirty softness; but the back had been lovingly stitched afresh with white cotton thread, which looked clean yet. It was an extraordinary find. Its title was, *An Inquiry into some Points of Seamanship*, by a man Towser, Towson—some such name—Master in His Majesty's Navy. The matter looked dreary reading enough, with illustrative diagrams and repulsive tables of figures, and the copy was sixty years old. I handled this amazing antiquity with the greatest possible tenderness, lest it should dissolve in my hands. Within, Towson or Towser was inquiring earnestly into the breaking strain of ships' chains and tackle, and other such matters. Not a very enthralling book; but at the first glance you could see there a singleness of intention, an honest concern for the right way of going to work, which made these humble pages, thought out so many years ago, luminous with another than a professional light. The simple old sailor, with his talk of chains and purchases, made me forget the jungle and the pilgrims in a delicious sensation of having come upon something unmistakably real. Such a book being there was wonderful enough; but still more astounding were the notes pencilled in the margin, and plainly referring to the text. I couldn't believe my eyes! They were in cipher! Yes, it looked like cipher. Fancy a man lugging with him a book of that description into this nowhere and studying it—and making notes—in cipher at that! It was an extravagant mystery.

"I had been dimly aware for some time of a worrying noise, and when I lifted my eyes I saw the wood-pile was gone, and the manager, aided by all the pilgrims, was shouting at me from the river-side. I slipped the book into my pocket. I assure you to leave off reading was like tearing myself away from the shelter of an old and solid friendship.

"I started the lame engine ahead. 'It must be this miserable trader—this intruder,' exclaimed the manager, looking back malevolently at the place we had left. 'He must be English,' I said. 'It will not save him from getting into trouble if he is not careful,' muttered the manager darkly. I observed with assumed innocence that no man was safe from trouble in this world.

"The current was more rapid now, the steamer seemed at her last gasp, the stern-wheel flopped languidly, and I caught myself listening on tip-toe for the next beat of the float, for in sober truth I expected the wretched thing to give up every moment. It was like watching the last flickers of a life. But still we crawled. Sometimes I would pick out a tree a little way ahead to measure our progress towards Kurtz by, but I lost it invariably before we got abreast. To keep the eyes so long on one thing was too much for human patience. The manager displayed a beautiful resignation. I fretted and fumed and took to arguing with myself whether or no I would talk openly with Kurtz; but before I could come to any conclusion it occurred to me that my speech or my silence, indeed any action of mine, would be a mere futility. What did it matter what any one

knew or ignored? What did it matter who was manager? One gets sometimes such a flash of insight. The
essentials of this affair lay deep under the surface, beyond my reach, and beyond my power of meddling.

"Towards the evening of the second day we judged
ourselves about eight miles from Kurtz's station. I
wanted to push on; but the manager looked grave, and
told me the navigation up there was so dangerous that
it would be advisable, the sun being very low already,
to wait where we were till next morning. Moreover, he
pointed out that if the warning to approach cautiously
were to be followed, we must approach in daylight—not
at dusk, or in the dark. This was sensible enough. Eight
miles meant nearly three hours' steaming for us, and I
could also see suspicious ripples at the upper end of the
reach. Nevertheless, I was annoyed beyond expression
at the delay, and most unreasonably, too, since one
night more could not matter much after so many
months. As we had plenty of wood, and caution was
the word, I brought up in the middle of the stream.
The reach was narrow, straight, with high sides like a
railway cutting. The dusk came gliding into it long
before the sun had set. The current ran smooth and
swift, but a dumb immobility sat on the banks. The
living trees, lashed together by the creepers and every
living bush of the undergrowth, might have been
changed into stone, even to the slenderest twig, to the
lightest leaf. It was not sleep—it seemed unnatural, like
a state of trance. Not the faintest sound of any kind
could be heard. You looked on amazed, and began to
suspect yourself of being deaf—then the night came
suddenly, and struck you blind as well. About three in
the morning some large fish leaped, and the loud splash

Reader's Supplement

to

HEART OF DARKNESS

JOSEPH CONRAD (1857–1924)

BIOGRAPHICAL BACKGROUND

Joseph Conrad (1857–1924) was originally named Józef Teodor Konrad Naeçz Korzeniowski, for this great English novelist was a Pole, born in Berdyczew, then under Russian domination. His father was a revolutionary and was exiled to Vologda when Conrad was five. Orphaned in 1869, the boy was sent to school in Cracow. He went to France in 1874. In Marseilles he became involved with the Carlist cause of Spain, smuggling arms by sea. In 1875 he sailed to Martinique, then to the West Indies, and in 1878 joined the English merchant service. He rose from third mate to first mate to master of his own ship (1886), and he became a naturalized subject of Britain, for he always loved that country where (as he said in his story *Youth*) "men and the sea interpenetrate, so to speak." Sailing between Singapore and Borneo, he picked up the knowledge of those exotic locales he was to put to good use in *Lord Jim* and *An Outcast of the Islands,* but it was his voyage to the Congo which was to make him a professional writer and give him the raw materials for *Heart of Darkness.*

In 1889 this adventurous spirit set out "for a stay of three years in the middle of Africa." After a visit with relatives that found something of an echo in *Heart of Darkness,* Conrad sailed from Bordeaux on the *Ville de Maceio,* a ship of the Compagnie des Chargeurs Réunis bound for places that even to a man of his wide experience must have been fascinating: Tenerife, Dakar, Konakri, Sierra Leone, Grand-Bassam, Kotonu, Libreville, Loango, Banana (at the mouth of the Congo River) and Boma (capital of the Congo Free State since 1886). From Boma he took a tiny steamboat to Matadi, and there be-

gan a journey as important to him as was André Gide's
venture into the Congo a generation later.

Matadi, about a hundred miles up the Congo River, had
one of the largest ocean harbors of Central Africa, but it
was truly an outpost of civilization. Conrad was to go
even deeper into the heart of the country. The real-life
background of *Heart of Darkness,* collected on that trip
along with a lot of navigation information about the
river, is contained in a couple of small black notebooks,
now in Harvard University's library. They tell of how he
arrived in Matadi in June, 1890—he had set out from
Bordeaux in May, 1890—and of his preparations to go
deeper into the interior. The journal describes his meeting
with Roger Casement* and, through him, a Mr. Under-
wood, the manager of an English factory (Halton &
Cookson) in Kalla Kalla. Such "commercial gentlemen"
as these, dealing in ivory and other things, were to give
the writer models and ideas. "Prominent characteristic of
the social life here," wrote Conrad: "people speaking ill
of each other." He listened to gossip, rumors, and kept
his eyes open. Everything was to be useful when he wrote
about the "Central Station." When he set out on a two-
hundred-mile trip on June 28 in company with M. Prosper
Harou of the État Indépendant du Congo Belge and thirty-
one bearers, Conrad kept notes. (*Heart of Darkness* speaks
of two hundred miles and sixty men.) The dead body of
a Backongo he saw at a camping place on July 3
("Shot?") became in his story "the body of a middle-aged
negro with a bullethole in his forehead," over which "a
white man in an unbuttoned uniform" was to stumble. The
ravines he crossed are described in the story and the
"shouts and drumming in the distant villages" he heard at

* [Sir] Roger Casement (1864–1916) later became British Consul in
the Congo Free State. He denounced Congo and Putumayo rubber
atrocities. Knighted in 1911, he was executed for treason the very
day Conrad died, for Casement landed in Ireland (from a German
submarine) to lead a rebellion.

night resonate in *Heart of Darkness* as "the tremor of far-off drums, sinking, swelling, a tremor vast, faint; a sound weird, appealing, suggestive and wild." A wrecked steamer (the *Florida*) was later to figure in the tale "at the bottom of the river." M. Harou, so ill he had to be carried, was also transferred from fact to fiction. A nineteen-day trip in reality became the fifteen-day trek to "the big river" and the "Central Station" in *Heart of Darkness*. Eventually Conrad was to go twice this far: from Stanley Pool to somewhere near Stanley Falls, or (in the book) into the very "heart of darkness" where he was to come upon "hints for nightmares."

When Conrad came to write *Heart of Darkness* for serialization in *Blackwood's Magazine* (February, March, and April, 1899), the experience all flooded back to him. His friend Robert Curle, who edited the notebooks we have mentioned, remembered "Conrad telling me that its 40,000 words occupied only about a month in writing. [This was remarkable] when we consider the painful, slow labor with which he usually composed." Of course, English was not Conrad's native language. Friends said that when he read his manuscripts aloud they realized that many of the words so brilliantly chosen Conrad had never heard, only read in books, and had no idea how to pronounce! "We can perceive how intensely vivid his memories of this experience must have been, and, to judge from the parallel passages, how intensely actual. But then the notebook only goes to prove the self-evident contention that much of Conrad's work is founded upon autobiographical remembrance," concluded Curle.

Of course Conrad made no attempt to hide the fact that his fiction grew out of fact. In his Author's Note to the book in which *Heart of Darkness* first appeared (with other tales, 1902), Conrad remarked that "it is well known that curious men go prying into all sorts of places (where they have no business) and come out from them with all kinds of spoil. This story, and one other, not in this volume, are all the spoil I brought out from the centre of Africa. . . ." The writer described *Heart of Darkness* candidly as "experience pushed a little (and only very little) beyond the actual facts of the case for the perfectly legitimate, I believe, purpose of bringing it home to the minds and bosoms of the readers." Elsewhere Conrad wrote that "work that aspires, however humbly, to the condition of art should carry its justification in every line." Here the "sinister resonance" in the writer's memory has been re-created in the reader's mind by the method of sticking very close to fact but sharpening points, where necessary, by deviating from actual events. *Heart of Darkness* is completely a work of art, a fiction, but—to use an image from Lord Byron—what the author has spun out of his own guts, the web of imagination, has been attached to very solid twigs of reality.

So vivid were the memories in Conrad's mind, or so determined was he to compel his imagination to make dry bones live, that he did not write with his notebooks before him. His wife testified that twice she had had to rescue these very notebooks from the wastepaper basket. The creative powers that were said to have been stirred to give us *Lord Jim*—an immensely complex study of character against a detailed background of the East, inspired simply because Conrad glimpsed a man in the street in a white suit and started to speculate on this total stranger—were permitted to work on the raw materials of the Congo experience. It is because Conrad's imagination was able to give such life to his memories, not because he took notes, that his works live in our imaginations and remain in our memories.

One can read Curle's edition of Conrad's Congo notebooks and from this "up river" diary (and a few hints in Conrad's autobiographical *A Personal Record*) find out something of the genesis of *Heart of Darkness*. But the real origin, and the real mystery, of *Heart of Darkness* lie deeper than "a feat of memory." "I insist not on the events," said Conrad of another story, "but on their effect on the persons of the tale." The origin and the significance of the book lie in the world of psychology, in the mind and the heart, where angst and alienation, morality and passion, guilt and expiation, horror and honor war for mastery. *Heart of Darkness* is not a great work just because Conrad actually was in the Congo, any more than *Victory* is a great work because he actually sailed in the East. However real the setting appears to be, it is *within* that we find "the horror, the horror" and the true meaning and genius of the tale.

All this is not to say that *Heart of Darkness* would have been written had Conrad not dared his African adventure. Indeed, had he not gone to the Congo he might not have published anything. His trip to the great river of Africa to command the S.S. *Roi des Belges* and all the hardships that befell him led to "a long, long illness and a very dismal convalescence," we are told. In fact, Africa spoiled his health and put an end to his membership in the "brotherhood of the sea" which he had long treasured. After the African adventure he had to retire from the merchant fleet. He had already become interested in writing. Even as he was sailing on the Congo River he had in his possession seven chapters of his first novel *(Almayer's Folly);* in fact, he almost lost them in the waters. When he was well enough again, he finished the book. The Congo adventure had launched him on the greatest adventure of his life: he was to be a writer. He published *Almayer's Folly* and began a whole new life at an age when most men are firmly settled into their careers. He married Jesse George and settled down, almost a recluse, at Ashford in Kent. There he produced two sons (Borys, born in 1898, and John Alexander, born in 1906) and the fiction that has gained him a permanent place in the first rank of British writers.

"Before the Congo," Conrad said to his friend Edward Garnett, "I was just a mere animal." He meant to express the fact that the Congo adventure had made him open his eyes and see, but also go beyond animals that see: to *think,* like a man, about the significance of what is seen. In time he wrote stories to help others to do the same things. In the famous Preface to *The Nigger of the "Narcissus,"* Conrad confessed that his first purpose was "to make you see, to make you feel that you are there, that you are having the experience yourself." Actually, being on the ground himself, must have helped Conrad to make the reader feel *he* is there, in the "heart of darkness." But Conrad also constantly strove to make the reader see the significance of what is seen, to understand the moral dilemmas of the characters whom he witnesses in action, to grasp the psychology of a secret agent, of an outcast of the islands, of the shadowy Mr. Kurtz. The Congo, and the illness that followed his trip there, made him reflect upon things, turned his eyes inward, forced him (in his own words) "to go through the ordeal of looking into it myself."

Edward Garnett, introducing his superb edition of *The Letters of Joseph Conrad, 1895–1924,* claims that, though we might think he had unusually broad experience to draw on and that the life of a sailor took him to many exotic ports, Conrad himself complained that, if not in the case of *Heart of Darkness* at least in a more general way, the sailor's life had much limited him!

That Conrad's memory had extraordinary wealth of observation to draw on, I had an illuminating proof in *Heart of Darkness.* Some time before he wrote this story of his Congo experience, he narrated it at length one morning while we were walking up and down under a row of Scotch firs that lead down to the [river] Cearne. I listened enthralled while he gave me in detail a very full synopsis of what he intended to write. To my surprise when I saw the printed version I found that about a third of the most striking incidents had been replaced by others of which he had said nothing at all. The effect of the written narrative was no less somber than the spoken, and the end was more consummate; but I regretted the omission of various scenes, one of which described the hero lying sick to death in a native hut, tended by an old negress who brought him water from day to day, when he had been abandoned by all the Belgians. "She saved my life," Conrad said, "the white men never came near me." When on several occasions in those early years I praised his psychological insight he questioned seriously whether he possessed such a power and deplored the lack of opportunities for intimate observation that a sailor's life had offered him. On one occasion in describing to him a terrible family tragedy of which I had been an eye-witness, Conrad became visibly ill-humored and at last cried out with exasperation, "Nothing of the kind has ever come my way! I have spent half my life knocking about in ships, only getting ashore between voyages. I know nothing, nothing! except from the outside. I have to guess at everything!"

The reader of *Heart of Darkness* will appreciate the fact that, even though Conrad experienced much of what he wrote about, he had "to guess at everything" as far as the *heart* of the story is concerned. The reader will certainly not agree that the author of *Heart of Darkness* knew "nothing, nothing! except from the outside," that he was right in turning aside compliments on "his psychological insight." What he has done with what *came his way* in the Congo is what makes *Heart of Darkness* so moving and so mysterious, so powerful, so haunting, not a mere adventure story or escape into an exotic setting but a profound psychological tale, a journey into self. And as Marlow said, "The most you can hope is some knowledge of yourself." *That,* and not actual details about Africa in a far-off and fearsome period, is the great gift that *Heart of Darkness* brings to the sensitive reader.

HISTORICAL BACKGROUND

From the *Natural History* of Pliny the Elder (23–79 A.D.) came a proverb: *Ex Africa semper aliquid nova.* There is always something new out of Africa. At the time that Joseph Conrad wrote *Heart of Darkness,* Africa was still bringing forth new wonders, though she was only half-explored, "a place of darkness," the Dark Continent, "one of the dark places of the earth," as Conrad put it.

In "Geography and Some Explorers" (in *Last Essays*), Conrad wrote of Africa and "the vilest scramble for loot that ever disfigured the history of human conscience and geographical exploration." Truly the sordid history of slave-trading and rapine, of the mad grabs for diamonds and gold and other treasures of Africa, made the continent perfect as a subject for Conrad. On the one hand the story was full of the Rider Haggard excitement and Rudyard Kipling melodrama of the outposts of empire that were basic ingredients in Conrad's work; and, on the other, the subject matter gave scope for Conrad's fundamental hatred of rapacious mercantilism ("the buying and selling crew who run this rotten show") and his essential moral questioning, his skepticism.

Within Africa, the Congo was one of the most exciting places at the time Conrad wrote. Even today we associate the Congo with violence—mercenary murderers having replaced the horrors of Leopold, King of the Belgians, cutting the hands off the natives in the last century. Then it was synonymous with mystery, evil, blood, cruelty and conquest. "The conquest of the earth," wrote Conrad, "which mostly means taking it away from those who have a different complexion or slightly flatter noses than ourselves, is not a pretty thing when you look into it too much." He looked into it and saw—the horror, the horror.

better understood by Conrad's readers because Mr. Kurtz was not an isolated case, because rumors had long since leaked to the outside world that in Darkest Africa and in other blank spaces on the maps of the nineteenth century more was going on than exploration or even exploitation. Men far from home and wandering in a moral desert reacted exactly as had the zealous hermits of the past: some became saints—and some went mad.

It is against this background of blood and glory, of fabulous achievements and frightening failures, of quest and questionable practices that Conrad's story is told.

Note: The page references on the following pages direct your attention to passages in the text (T for Top of page, M for Middle, and B for Bottom).

PICTORIAL BACKGROUND

The sea-reach of the Thames stretched before us like the beginning of an interminable waterway. In the offing the sea and the sky were welded together without a joint, and in the luminous space the tanned sails of the barges drifting up with the tide seemed to stand still in red clusters of canvas sharply peaked. . . . (p. 1M)

A SCENE AT THE LONDON DOCKS
Whistler

"*An eerie feeling came over me. She seemed uncanny and fateful. Often far away there I thought of these two, guarding the door of Darkness, knitting black wool as for a warm pall, one introducing, introducing continuously to the unknown, the other scrutinizing the cheery and foolish faces with unconcerned old eyes.*" (p. 14T)

A SECRETARY KNITTING DURING A LULL—1909

"*One thing more remained to do—say good-bye to my excellent aunt. I found her triumphant. I had a cup of tea—the last decent cup of tea for many days—and in a room that most soothingly looked just as you would expect a lady's drawing-room to look, we had a long quiet chat by the fireside.*" (p. 16T)

TEA TIME IN LONDON—LATE 1800's

"*It was upward of thirty days before I saw the mouth of the big river. We anchored off the seat of the government. But my work would not begin till some two hundred miles farther on. So as soon as I could I made a start for a place thirty miles higher up.*

"*I had my passage on a little sea-going steamer.*" (p. 20T)

BOMA, CAPITAL OF THE CONGO FREE STATE—1893

"*A slight clinking behind me made me turn my head. Six black men advanced in a file, toiling up the path. They walked erect and slow, balancing small baskets full of earth on their heads, and the clink kept time with their footsteps. Black rags were wound round their loins and the short ends behind waggled to and fro like tails.*" (p. 21B)

CHAINED AFRICAN SLAVES—LATE 1800's

"*Next day I left that station at last, with a caravan of sixty men, for a two-hundred-mile tramp.*

"*No use telling you much about that. Paths, paths, everywhere; a stamped-in network of paths spreading over the empty land, through long grass, through burnt grass, through thickets down and up chilly ravines. . . .*" (p. 28M)

AFRICAN SAFARI—LATE 1800's

"*The word 'ivory' rang in the air, was whispered, was sighed. You would think they were praying to it. A taint of imbecile rapacity blew through it all, like a whiff from some corpse. By Jove! I've never seen anything so unreal in my life. And outside, the silent wilderness surrounding this cleared speck on the earth. . . .*" (p. 34T)

IVORY BEING BROUGHT IN BY THE NATIVES

"*But suddenly, as we struggled round a bend, there would be a glimpse of rush walls, of peaked grass-roofs, a burst of yells, a whirl of black limbs, a mass of hands clapping, of feet stamping, of bodies swaying, of eyes rolling, under the droop of heavy and motionless foliage.*" (p. 54B)

NATIVE VILLAGE OF "GRASS-ROOFS"

"One of my hungry and forbearing friends was sounding in the bows just below me. This steamboat was exactly like a decked scow. On the deck, there were two little teak-wood houses, with doors and windows. The boiler was in the fore-end, and the machinery right astern. Over the whole there was a light roof. . . ." (p. 68B)

A STEAMBOAT IN AFRICAN WATERS—LATE 1800's

"I saw a face amongst the leaves on the level with my own, looking at me very fierce and steady; and then suddenly, as though a veil had been removed from my eyes, I made out, deep in the tangled gloom, naked breasts, arms, legs, glaring eyes. . . . The twigs shook, swayed, and rustled, the arrows flew out of them. . . ." (p. 70T)

CANNIBALS WITH NATIVE WEAPONS

"*The man had rolled on his back and stared straight up at me; both his hands clutched that cane. It was the shaft of a spear that, either thrown or lunged through the opening, had caught him in the side just below the ribs; the blade had gone in out of sight, after making a frightful gash. . . .*"

(p. 72T)

AFRICAN NATIVES ATTACK WITH SPEARS

"The start back I had given was really nothing but a move-ment of surprise. I had expected to see a knob of wood there, you know. I returned deliberately to the first I had seen—and there it was, black, dried, sunken, with closed eyelids,—a head that seemed to sleep at the top of that pole. . . ." (p. 91M)

SHRUNKEN HEAD BEFORE BEING MOUNTED

"*Suddenly round the corner of the house a group of men appeared, as though they had come up from the ground. They waded waist-deep in the grass, in a compact body, bearing an improvised stretcher in their midst. Instantly, in the emptiness of the landscape, a cry arose whose shrillness pierced the still air like a sharp arrow. . . .*" (p. 94T)

NATIVES WITH IMPROVISED LITTER

"I glanced back. We were within thirty yards from the nearest fire. A black figure stood up, strode on long black legs, waving long black arms, across the glow. It had horns—antelope horns, I think—on its head. Some sorcerer, some witch-man, no doubt; it looked fiendlike enough." (p. 104M)

AFRICAN "SORCERER"

"*Did he live his life again in every detail of desire, temptation, and surrender during that supreme moment of complete knowledge? He cried in a whisper at some image, at some vision—he cried out twice, a cry that was no more than a breath—*

"*'The horror! The horror!'*" (p. 111T)

PART OF THE HORROR—HUMAN DEBRIS

"*She came forward, all in black, with a pale head, floating towards me in the dusk. She was in mourning. It was more than a year since his death, more than a year since the news came; she seemed as though she would remember and mourn for ever. She took both my hands in hers and murmured, 'I had heard you were coming.'*" (p. 118T)

MOURNING WRAP—1890's

VISUAL GLOSSARY

1–yawl (p. 1T)   2–sarcophagus (p. 118B)
3–toga (p. 6M)

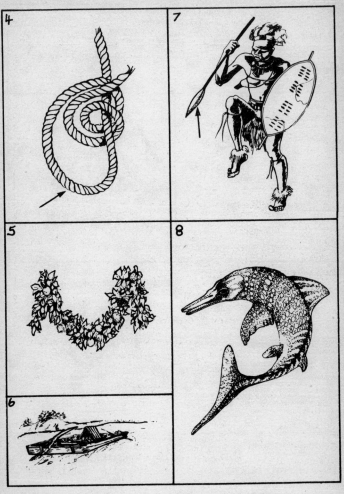

4—bight (p. 21B)   6—scow (p. 68B)
5—festoon (p. 45T)   7—assegais (p. 35M)
        8—ichthyosaurus (p. 45M)

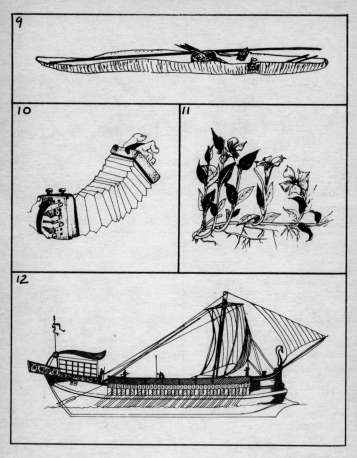

9–dugout (p. 48B) 11–creepers (p. 60B)
10–concertina (p. 6T) 12–trireme (p. 5B)

LITERARY ALLUSIONS AND NOTES

Thames . . . Gravesend (p. 1B):
> *Heart of Darkness* is, of course, an African story, but it is well to remember that Marlow tells it to a group of his London friends on board the *Nellie,* anchored in the Thames, the river that flows through London to the North Sea. Gravesend is a port quite near the open sea on the southern bank of the Thames.

Sir Francis Drake . . . Sir John Franklin . . . the *Golden Hind* . . . the Queen's Highness . . . the Erebus and Terror (p. 3B):
> Marlow is referring to famous expeditions and voyages of exploration which had started out from the spot on the Thames where he is now telling the story of his expedition. Drake (1540?–1596), a naval officer in the service of "the Queen's Highness," Elizabeth I of England, was the first Englishman to circumnavigate the earth. He set out in December 1577 in five ships to raid Spanish ports and Spanish ships in South America. After many adventures and the loss of four of his ships, he sailed in his remaining ship, the *Golden Hind,* up the Pacific coast of North America, sought but failed to find a waterway across the continent to the Atlantic, claimed part of the western coast of the New World for Queen Elizabeth, and then sailed westward across the Pacific. After visiting a number of islands in the South Pacific, he rounded the southern tip of Africa at the Cape of Good Hope and, laden with treasure, arrived back in England in September 1580. Franklin (1786–1847), who had done a great deal of exploring in Canada, set out in 1845 in two ships, the *Erebus* and the *Terror,* to search for the Northwest Passage, but he, his men, and his ships were never seen again.

Deptford . . . Greenwich . . . Erith (p. 4T):
> These are seaports on the Thames closer to the open sea than London is. As a seaman, Marlow would be familiar with the less important ports, as well as with the larger ones.

"interlopers" ... East India fleets (p. 4T):
Elizabeth I had granted the British East India Company a charter which gave it a monopoly on trade with the East. In time, however, a good many independent shippers—"interlopers"—began to engage in trade with the East. Notice that these comments are of the sort that would be made by a professional, one quite familiar with the world of shipping and of trade.

Falernian wine (p. 6T) ... Ravenna (p. 6M):
Not merely a sailor, but like his creator, Conrad, a highly educated one, Marlow refers to ancient history in the manner of a man who has done a good deal of reading. Falernian wine was an ancient Roman vintage celebrated in the poems of Horace (Quintus Horatius Flaccus, 65–8 B.C.). Ravenna was the chief ancient Roman naval port in the North Adriatic.

Buddha (p. 7T):
One of the traditional statues of Buddha (563–483 B.C.), the founder of the Buddhist religion, is that of a seated, cross-legged figure with hands clasped in front or with one hand raised, palm outward, as if in gesture. The lotus flower, often held by the statue, is a symbol of the Buddha. What effect does Conrad achieve by comparing Marlow to a Buddha?

Fleet Street (p. 9B):
Mentioning Fleet Street, one of the busiest in London, serves as a contrast in Marlow's mind between the bustling center of civilization as he knows it and the African wilderness he is telling his friends about.

Ave! ... Morituri te salutant. **(p. 14T):**
Latin for "Hail! They who are about to die salute you"—the cry of the Roman gladiators to the emperor. The significance of Marlow's remark is in the next sentence: "Not many of those she looked at ever saw her again—not half, by a long way."

Du calme, du calme. Adieu. **(p. 16T):**
"Take it easy, don't get excited, be calm. Good-bye."

papier-mâché Mephistopheles (p. 39T):
Papier-mâché is a mixture of paper pulp, glue, rosin, clay

or similar materials and can be shaped into various forms. Mephistopheles is a legendary devil best known in literature as the tempter in the medieval Faust stories. Marlow is really calling the brickmaker a fake devil or manipulator.

on tip-toe for the next beat of the float (p. 59M):
A float is a hollow metallic ball, usually at the end of a rod or lever, which floats on top of the water in a tank or a boiler and which, as it rises and falls, opens and shuts a valve which regulates the level of the water. A similar device, often in the shape of a horseshoe rather than a ball, is used to regulate the supply of gasoline in the carburetor of a gasoline engine. It was the float in his engine that was making Marlow nervous.

a harlequin (p. 82B):
Harlequin, lover of Columbine, was a comic character in Italian pantomime, later in the English Punch and Judy puppet shows, and eventually in the comic theater of most European countries. Because Harlequin traditionally wore multicolored costumes, Marlow labeled the colorfully be-patched Russian seaman a harlequin.

the thunderbolts of that pitiful Jupiter (p. 95M):
Since Kurtz, who was worshiped as a god by the natives, was ill, he could not very well use his weapons, hence the mildly ironic designation of him as a pitiful Jupiter, the Roman god whose weapons were thunderbolts.

satanic litany (p. 107M):
To Marlow, the incomprehensible sounds the natives were making seemed to be a litany, a prayer of supplication to the devil—Satan, the archfiend, once an archangel, who was cast out of heaven for disobedience and pride.

CRITICAL EXCERPTS

Selected from the hundreds of articles, biographies, and volumes of criticism written about Joseph Conrad, here are some excerpts that should prove challenging to you. We have included page references to *Heart of Darkness,* indicated in parentheses, so that you can review sample passages to help you decide whether to accept or reject the quoted comments.

No matter how imaginative, even unreal, a tale may be, its readers are invariably curious as to how closely the incidents in the story parallel those in the private life of its author. *Heart of Darkness* seems made to order for such readers, for it is a reflection, a re-creation, of one of the crucial experiences in the life of the man who wrote it. Here are Joseph Conrad's own words:

1. *It was in 1868, when nine years old or thereabouts, that while looking at a map of Africa of the time and putting my finger on the blank space then representing the unsolved mystery of that continent, I said to myself with absolute assurance and an amazing audacity which are no longer in my character now:*
   "When I grow up I shall go there.*"*

> *A Personal Record,* Joseph Conrad,
> J. M. Dent & Sons, 1912.

In 1890, when Conrad was still a comparatively young man —aged thirty-three— he was given the opportunity to fulfill his boyhood ambition and make his dreamed-of journey to the Congo.

2. *Conrad's command of a Congo river steamer had finally been put through—again he was to replace a captain who had died—and on May 6, 1890, he left for Africa.*
   Sailing on a French steamer from Bordeaux, he arrived at

Matadi in the Belgian Congo on June 12, 1890. Construction of the railroad had just begun and he faced a walk of more than two hundred miles to reach his steamer at Stanley Falls. . . .

Conrad arrived in the Congo five years after Leopold II of Belgium had organized his private "International Association for the Exploration and Civilization of the Congo," when that part of the world was witnessing the most brutal period of exploitation history ever knew. The savagery of Leopold's treatment of the Africans created an international scandal and in 1908 he was forced to relinquish the area that had made him so fabulously rich. . . .

The company's agent at the outpost was a Frenchman, Georges Antoine Klein. He had been in the Congo less than two years . . . when he succumbed to tropical fever. Carried by stretcher on board the Roi des Belges, *he died on the downstream journey.*

Eight years after meeting Klein at Stanley Falls, Conrad wrote him into Heart of Darkness *as Kurtz.*

> *The Thunder and the Sunshine, a Biography of Joseph Conrad*, Jerry Allen, G. P. Putnam, 1958.

Notice the parallel between Conrad's career and Marlow's adventures. Marlow got his command after the death of Fresleven (p. 10B). Marlow, too, left for Africa in a French steamer (p. 17M), taking thirty days to arrive at the "mouth of the big river" (p. 20T). Here he learned that his "work would not begin till some two hundred miles farther on" (p. 20T) and, after waiting at the station for ten days (p. 26M), he traveled overland for fifteen days (p. 30T) before arriving at the Central Station where he could take command of his boat. From almost the very beginning of his arrival in Africa, Marlow got the opportunity to observe what Conrad had seen of Leopold's exploitation of the Africans: the man-of-war (on which men were dying of fever at the rate of three a day), "firing into a continent" (p. 19T), the chain gang (p. 21B), and the grove of dying men (pp. 24T–25T).

Apparently, however, Conrad's African experience was to have a much more significant effect on his life than merely to provide him with background and material for one of his tales. His biographer, G. Jean-Aubry, reveals some interesting details:

3. *The immediate consequence of this journey to the Congo was—as Conrad has said himself—a long, long illness and a dreary convalescence. Conrad's health was affected during all the rest of his life by this African expedition. . . . The illness which he brought back from the Congo, by limiting his physical activity and confining him to his room for several months, obliged him to withdraw into himself, to call up those memories with which his life, though he was only thirty-three, was already extraordinarily full, and to try to estimate their value both from the human and the literary point of view. . . . It may be said that Africa killed Conrad the sailor and strengthened Conrad the novelist.*

> *Joseph Conrad, Life and Letters,* G. Jean-Aubry, Doubleday, Page & Co., 1927.

Edward Garnett, one of Joseph Conrad's closest friends—in fact, he was the publisher's editor of a good many of Conrad's works—confirms what has been said by Jean-Aubry.

4. *I agree with M. Jean-Aubry that Conrad's Congo experiences were the turning point in his mental life and that its effect on him determined his transformation from a sailor to a writer. . . . The sinister voice of the Congo with its murmuring undertone of human fatuity, baseness, and greed had swept away the generous illusions of his youth and had left him gazing into the heart of an immense darkness.*

> "Introduction" to *Letters from Conrad, 1895–1924*, Edward Garnett, Editor, Nonesuch Press, 1928.

A striking parallel between Conrad's career and *Heart of*

Darkness is, of course, the almost fatal sickness that struck Marlow after the death of Kurtz (pp. 112T–113B). The book, however, is much more than a thinly veiled autobiographical sketch; if it were not, this would be a pointless story. The emerging writer was reaching back into his past to re-create experiences that would reflect the development of his philosophy of life, his understanding of people with their basic drives, their weaknesses and strengths.

What Conrad is trying to say in *Heart of Darkness*—the purpose or theme of his story—is a subject which has fascinated a good many critics.

5. Heart of Darkness . . . *was of European importance. In it, Conrad, drawing on his own experiences in the Congo, had put in a long short-story what scores of travelers and investigators affirmed about the enslavement of the Congo peoples by their Belgian masters. But what reports . . . cannot do,* Heart of Darkness *did, by catching the infinite shades of deterioration in the white man's morale when he is freed from European restraint and planted down in the tropics to make profit out of black subject races.*

> "Introductory Essay" to *Conrad's Prefaces,* Edward Garnett, J. M. Dent & Sons, 1937.

6. *The autobiographical basis of the narrative is well known, and its introspective bias obvious; this is Conrad's longest journey into self. But it is well to remember that* Heart of Darkness *is also other if more superficial things: a sensitive and vivid travelogue and a comment on "the vilest scramble for loot that ever disfigured the history of human conscience and geographical exploration."* . . . Heart of Darkness *thus has its important side, as an angry document on absurd and brutal exploitation. . . . Conrad was reacting to the humanitarian pretenses of some of the looters precisely as the novelist today reacts to the moralisms of cold war propaganda. Then it was ivory that poured from the heart of darkness; now it is uranium. Conrad shrewdly recognized . . . that deception is*

most sinister when it becomes self-deception and the propagandist takes seriously his own fiction.

> Conrad the Novelist, Albert J.
> Guérard, Harvard University Press,
> 1958, 1965.

The "humanitarian pretenses" mentioned by Guérard are depicted in a number of places in the story. Possibly the most dramatic is Kurtz's pamphlet written for the International Society for the Suppression of Savage Customs (p. 78T) and the random phrases Marlow quotes from it and says about it (p. 78M): " '. . . we can exert a power for good practically unbounded' "; "august Benevolence"; "burning noble words"; "moving appeal to every altruistic sentiment." In analyzing the purpose of the book, the reader should try to determine whether Conrad was mainly concerned with expressing his own reactions to violence, cruelty, and greed or building primarily a sociological document that exposed the inhumanity behind colonial exploitation.

In the excerpt which follows, a critic introduces a rather disturbing suggestion about at least one of the purposes Conrad had in describing the role played by the English in the brutal struggle for ivory.

7. *Although Marlow admits that English conquest, like all others, "means the taking [the earth] away from those who have a different complexion or slightly flatter noses than ourselves," he claims that the English form is redeemed by an idea: "An idea at the back of it; not a sentimental pretence but an idea; and an unselfish belief in the idea—something you can set up, and bow down before, and offer a sacrifice to. . . ." [p. 7B]*

All critics have read this astonishing passage as a straightforward, unambiguous apology for British imperialism, spoken from Conrad's heart through Marlow's mouth. No one seems to hear the reverberations of Marlow's bitter emphasis later on figures of religious devotion, especially the worship of ideas. He will himself finally say that he had to lay the ghost of Kurtz's "gifts" with a lie [p. 75M], but it is left to the reader to perceive that Marlow must kill off a part of his own self-knowledge with lies in order to save the "beautiful world" of British civilization along with the beautiful world of Kurtz's Intended.

> *The Political Novels of Joseph Conrad, a Critical Study,* Eloise Knapp Hay, The University of Chicago Press, 1963.

To understand the point that Eloise Knapp Hay is making, you must establish in your own mind the connection between the lie Marlow tells Kurtz's intended (p. 123B) and the saving of the "beautiful world" of British civilization. It is important for the reader to determine the extent to which Conrad was trying to cover up for his English compatriots and their colonial practices.

Marlow's relationship to Kurtz is, of course, another key to understanding *Heart of Darkness*. A number of critics have concerned themselves with analyzing both men.

8. *Kurtz conceives of himself as a civilizer instead of as an exploiter of the natives, although he nevertheless succeeds in extracting more ivory from the natives than does any other trader. . . . Marlow finds Kurtz crawling on his hands and knees towards a savage and turbulent ceremonial gathering. The spiritual contest which takes place at this point between Marlow and Kurtz is the heart of* Heart of Darkness. *Marlow wrestles with Kurtz like Jacob wrestled with the Angel . . . Kurtz is torn between two great losses. If he goes back to the savages, he will be cut off forever from his civilized European connections. . . . He will be accepting once and for all time the ascendancy in his own nature of elements which enslave him: the impulse to despotic life-and-death power over an empire of black African savages; the impulse to bask and loll in the abject worship accorded him as a god. . . . This is what his great pretensions to civilize the natives have dwindled*

in'o: self-adulation. The natives have suborned him by their adulation.

> *Joseph Conrad: A Study in Nonconformity,* Osborn Andreas, Philosophical Library, 1959.

9. *Kurtz knew of the blackness, the darkness, which is at the heart of humanity; he knew the depths to which man is capable of sinking; he knew that the light of civilization could not penetrate this darkness, could only emphasize its sinister pervasiveness; and worst of all, he knew that he had turned away from this feeble light, so that he had been enveloped in the darkness which is at the heart of every man. He had, in the end, "pronounced a judgment upon the adventures of his soul on this earth." Kurtz was a remarkable man because he had perceived this darkness, and since Marlow had vicariously partaken of Kurtz's revelation, he was the only person associated with the agent who could come near to penetrating the meaning of Kurtz's summing up: "The horror! the horror!"*

> "The Light and the Dark; Imagery and Thematic Development in Conrad's *Heart of Darkness*," Wilfred S. Dowden, *Rice Institute Pamphlet,* April 1957.

10. *This trip fulfilled [Marlow's] boyhood dream of traveling to the center of Africa, but it also replaced that dream with a nightmare from which he never wholly recovered. His African experience revealed certain things about himself which he would have preferred not to have learned, and he was so maimed by his revulsion against the savage life he found there that he hardly ever felt at home in civilized society thereafter. He fell in love with savagery but remained defeated and stricken by reason of his inability to embrace and accept the object of his love.*

> *Joseph Conrad: A Study in Nonconformity,* Osborn Andreas.

11. *Substantially and in its central emphasis* Heart of Dark-

ness *concerns Marlow . . . and his journey toward and through certain facets or potentialities of self. . . . At a material and rather superficial level, the journey is through the temptation of atavism. It is a record of "remote kinship" with the "wild and passionate uproar," of a "trace of response" [p. 55B] to it, of a final rejection of the "fascination of the abomination." [p. 7T] . . . Marlow's temptation is made concrete through his exposure to Kurtz, a white man and sometime idealist who had fully responded to the wilderness: a potential and fallen self. . . .*

> **Conrad the Novelist**, Albert J. Guérard.

12. *Throughout, Marlow pronounces the kinship between the howling, screaming Congolese and the rest of humanity, climaxed by the look given him by the dying Negro helmsman, a look creating a "subtle bond" between them.*

> *Joseph Conrad: Giant in Exile*, Leo Gurko, The Macmillan Company, 1962.

13. *Only after Marlow passes his final test, his brush with death, does the full significance of Kurtz come to him. Kurtz's last cry takes us to the meaning of the whole African adventure for Marlow. . . . For Marlow sees that Kurtz's cry is more than self-knowledge, more than insight into the depths of his own evil. It is an insight into the potentialities of all men. . . . It is for Marlow a terrible illumination, for in Kurtz, Marlow discovers not simply one man become evil, but a universal possibility. Deprived of this insulation of society, the protecting surface, faced with the terrible challenge, we discover we are free; the very fact is terrifying, for in that choice lies the unpredictable, even the Kurtzian.*

> "Marlow's Quest," Jerome Thale, *University of Toronto Quarterly*, July 1955.

14. *Marlow's moral position, though seeming plainer than it is, is emphatic. Approving fidelity, duty, discipline, and order,*

*of which rivets, navigation, and light seem symbolic, he abhors
dark disorder. Morality involves choice: Marlow's, however,
is not between light and dark, but between kinds of dark.*

> "Apology for Marlow," W. Y. Tin-
> dall, in *From Jane Austen to Joseph
> Conrad*, R. C. Rathburn and M.
> Steinman, Jr., Editors, University of
> Minnesota Press, 1959.

How did you see Kurtz? Do you agree that Kurtz was
simply a man whose head was turned by power or do you
agree with Dowden that it is not so much Kurtz's wickedness
that destroys him as it is his own knowledge of how evil he
is? One thing is clear. To most critics, Kurtz is a badly flawed,
a psychologically crippled person. Is he that to you, or is he
simply a greedy, albeit brilliant, wretch who ultimately got
what he deserved?

To many commentators Kurtz is comparatively easy to
characterize as hollow or weak or evil, but Marlow is much
more difficult to pin down. Whether he was, as Guérard says,
one who was deeply troubled by the dissatisfactions he discovered within himself and with the civilization he could no
longer tolerate comfortably, he was most certainly a per-
manently unhappy person as a result of his African experiences. You may, possibly, be more deeply attracted to the
ideas of Thale, to whom Marlow represents a human being
who discovers how terrible it is to be free—for free men make
choices in life—or of Tindall, who thinks that Marlow, though
free to choose, could choose only between evils.

One rather startling view of the impact of the book through
one of its central characters was presented by H. L. Mencken:

15. *The exact point of the story of Kurtz, in* Heart of Darkness, *is that it is pointless, that Kurtz's death is as meaningless
as his life, that the moral of such a story is a wholesale nega-
tion of all morals. . . . He [Conrad] neither protests nor
punishes; he merely smiles and pities.*

> *A Book of Prefaces,* H. L. Menck-
> en, Alfred A. Knopf, Inc., 1945.

Notice, first of all, that the pointlessness which Mencken is speaking of is not emptiness or lack of merit or lack of interest. Such attributes would make reading *Heart of Darkness* a waste of time. On the contrary, Mencken read the book with pleasure and admiration and wrote about it with enthusiasm. What Mencken is talking about is philosophical pointlessness, that of the futility of man's actions, the indifference of the fates as to whether or not his character or his actions are good or bad.

If you agree with Mencken that Conrad's *Heart of Darkness* is—from this "philosophical" viewpoint—pointless, it might be well to ask yourself a second time whether you really think that Conrad takes no attitudes, expresses no point of view, chooses no sides, remains aloof from all of man's struggles on earth.

Other critics who seek to assess the significance of *Heart of Darkness*, who try to estimate what Conrad succeeded in doing with his story, do so in terms of the influence on each other of Kurtz and Marlow as well as their relationship to the world about them.

16. *Both Kurtz and Marlow sat in judgment on the society from which they sprang, but Kurtz died because he condemned and rejected that society while Marlow lived because the loss of his esteem for his group did not prevent him from working out a* modus vivendi *that kept open at least some of the channels of communication between himself and the group to which he belonged.*

> *Joseph Conrad: A Study in Nonconformity,* Osborn Andreas.

Compare the remarks of Andreas with those made by Marlow (pp. 113B–114T): "I found myself . . . resenting the sight of people. . . . They trespassed upon my thoughts. They were intruders whose knowledge of life was to me an irritating pretence, because I felt so sure they could not possibly know the things I knew."

17. *This brings out the radical difference in the effect that the wilderness has on Kurtz and on Marlow. Kurtz succumbs totally to the power of the wilderness and only emerges momentarily at the end to full awareness of his experience, whereas Marlow is forced to make a limited concession to the wilderness but preserves his moral being because he is not "hollow at the core." [p. 92M] The irony that it was morally right for Marlow to make this concession is an essential ingredient of Conrad's view of life. In a corrupt world one is bound to commit a corrupt act. Tragedy would have been the result of telling the truth; the "salvation of another soul" was at stake.*

Joseph Conrad, Jocelyn Baines, Weidenfeld and Nicolson, 1960.

Notice how two perceptive critics can each emphasize different aspects of a situation. To Andreas the important thing is the death of Kurtz because of his condemnation and rejection of civilized society. To Baines, however, it is much more significant that at the moment of death Kurtz's cry, in the words of Conrad, "was an affirmation, a moral victory." Both commentators agree that Marlow was never the same man again.

It would be difficult to find a writer whose English prose style has been praised as extravagantly as Conrad's; yet it would be a mistake to assume that for *Heart of Darkness* this praise has been unanimous. What follows is a small sampling.

18. *Is there not also a central obscurity, something noble, heroic, beautiful, inspiring, half a dozen great books, but obscure, obscure? . . . the secret casket of his genius contains a vapor rather than a jewel.*

"Albinger Harvest," E. M. Forster, in *The Great Tradition*, F. R. Leavis, New York University Press, 1964.

19. *There are, however, places in* Heart of Darkness *where*

*we become aware of comment as an . . . intrusion, at times
an exasperating one. Hadn't he, we find ourselves asking,
overworked "inscrutable," "inconceivable," "unspeakable" and
that kind of word already?—yet still they recur. Is anything
added to the oppressive mysteriousness of the Congo by such
sentences as: "It was the stillness of an implacable force
brooding over an inscrutable intention"? The same vocabulary,
the same adjectival insistence upon inexpressible and incomprehensible mystery, is applied to the evocation of human
profundities and spiritual horrors. . . . The actual effect is
not to magnify but rather to muffle. . . . Conrad must here
stand convicted of borrowing the arts of the magazine writer
. . . in order to impose on his readers and on himself, for
thrilled response, a "significance" that is merely an emotional
insistence on the presence of what he can't produce. . . . He
is intent on making a virtue of not knowing what he means.*

The Great Tradition, F. R. Leavis.

20. *Conrad's stories are distinguished for certain qualities of
narrative art, notably a tendency . . . to postpone the crisis
and defeat expectation. The result is to concentrate the force
of the situation in a total effect of explosive intensity. . . .
Again, he deals with characters of a powerful and bizarre
originality, tested by strange conditions and extraordinary
events. Above all, he handles scene with wonderful effect to
create that significant and influential medium which we call
atmosphere. . . . The Heart of Darkness . . . is a magnificent
example of atmosphere determining the unity and total effect
of the short story. The heavy tropical air of equatorial Africa
broods like a miasma over the monstrous and uncouth works
of nature, twisting humanity itself into similar forms of atrocious inhumanity.*

A History of English Literature,
William Vaughan Moody and Rob-
ert M. Lovett, Seventh Edition,
Charles Scribner and Sons, 1956.

21. *In the first place, Conrad set no emphasis on plot. Character and atmosphere to Conrad were everything, plot nothing.*

Secondly, though he is a verbose writer . . . his verbosity . . . is a new and gorgeous verbosity. It is the sublime verbosity of the poet. . . . Conrad set out to impress us, and did impress us, by words that were like paint, by a style that was dau̇ ed on the page with prodigious liberality, in gorgeous and somber overtones, the sort of style which in fact had never been seen in English literature before and has never been seen since.

> "Joseph Conrad and Thomas Hardy," H. E. Bates, in *The English Novelists,* Derek Verschoyle, Editor, Harcourt Brace and Company, 1936.

To arrive at your own estimate of Conrad's style—whether it is rather verbose and frequently diffuse or "sublime and poetic in its intensity"—you would do well to examine the following passages:

- —"The old river . . ." (p. 3M)
- —"Watching a coast as it slips by . . ." (p. 17M)
- —". . . there she was, incomprehensible, firing into a continent." (p. 19T)
- —"They were dying slowly . . ." (p. 24T)
- —". . . this papier-mâché Mephistopheles . . ." (p. 39T)
- —"Going up that river . . ." (p. 51M)
- —"Trees, trees, millions of trees . . ." (p. 54T)
- —". . . the playful paw-strokes of the wilderness . . ." (p. 64B)
- —"Perhaps you will think it passing strange . . ." (p. 79B)
- —"I tried to break the spell . . ." (p. 105M)

Whatever your final judgment of *Heart of Darkness* as a story or Conrad as writer, you will doubtless agree that the classic virtues of a literary creation—richness of imagery, depth of understanding, virtuosity in language, universality of concepts and ideas—are present in abundance in the book. It follows, then, that the author merits your further attention, in some of his other works, if only to test your ability to appreciate the genius of one of the great masters of English prose.

made me jump as though a gun had been fired. When the sun rose there was a white fog, very warm and clammy, and more blinding than the night. It did not shift or drive; it was just there, standing all round you like something solid. At eight or nine, perhaps, it lifted as a shutter lifts. We had a glimpse of the towering multitude of trees, of the immense matted jungle, with the blazing little ball of the sun hanging over it—all perfectly still—and then the white shutter came down again, smoothly, as if sliding in greased grooves. I ordered the chain, which we had begun to heave in, to be paid out again. Before it stopped running with a muffled rattle, a cry, a very loud cry as of infinite desolation, soared slowly in the opaque air. It ceased. A complaining clamour, modulated in savage discords, filled our ears. The sheer unexpectedness of it made my hair stir under my cap. I don't know how it struck the others: to me it seemed as though the mist itself had screamed, so suddenly, and apparently from all sides at once, did this tumultuous and mournful uproar arise. It culminated in a hurried outbreak of almost intolerably excessive shrieking, which stopped short, leaving us stiffened in a variety of silly attitudes, and obstinately listening to the nearly as appalling and excessive silence. 'Good God! What is the meaning——' stammered at my elbow one of the pilgrims,—a little fat man, with sandy hair and red whiskers, who wore sidespring boots, and pink pyjamas tucked into his socks. Two others remained open-mouthed a whole minute, then dashed into the little cabin, to rush out incontinently and stand darting scared glances, with Winchesters at 'ready' in their hands. What we could see was just the steamer we were on, her outlines blurred as though she had been on the point of dissolving, and a misty strip of water, perhaps two feet broad, around her—and that was all. The rest of the world was nowhere, as far as our eyes and ears were concerned. Just nowhere. Gone, disappeared; swept off without leaving a whisper or a shadow behind.

"I went forward, and ordered the chain to be hauled in short, so as to be ready to trip the anchor and move the steamboat at once if necessary. 'Will they attack?' whispered an awed voice. 'We will be all butchered in this fog,' murmured another. The faces twitched with the strain, the hands trembled slightly, the eyes forgot to wink. It was very curious to see the contrast of expressions of the white men and of the black fellows of our crew, who were as much strangers to that part of the river as we, though their homes were only eight hundred miles away. The whites, of course greatly discomposed, had besides a curious look of being painfully shocked by such an outrageous row. The others had an alert, naturally interested expression; but their faces were essentially quiet, even those of the one or two who grinned as they hauled at the chain. Several exchanged short, grunting phrases, which seemed to settle the matter to their satisfaction. Their headman, a young, broad-chested black, severely draped in dark-blue fringed cloths, with fierce nostrils and his hair all done up artfully in oily ringlets, stood near me. 'Aha!' I said, just for good fellowship's sake. 'Catch 'im,' he snapped, with a bloodshot widening of his eyes and a flash of sharp teeth—'catch 'im. Give 'im to us.' 'To you, eh?' I asked; 'what would you do with them?' 'Eat 'im!' he said, curtly, and, leaning his elbow on the rail, looked out into the fog in a dignified and profoundly pensive attitude. I would no doubt have been properly horrified, had it not occurred to me that he and his chaps must be very hungry: that they must have been growing increasingly hungry for at least this month past. They had been engaged for six months (I don't think a single one of them had any clear idea of time, as we at the end of countless ages have. They still belonged to the beginnings of time—had no inherited experience to teach them as it were), and of course, as long as there was a piece of paper written over in accordance with some farcical law or other made down the river, it didn't enter anybody's head to trouble how they would live. Certainly they had brought with them some rotten hippo-meat, which couldn't have lasted very long, anyway, even if the pilgrims hadn't, in the midst of a shocking hullabaloo, thrown a considerable quantity of it overboard. It looked like a high-handed proceeding; but it was really a case of legitimate self-defence. You can't breathe dead hippo waking, sleeping, and eating, and at the same time keep your precarious grip on existence. Besides that, they had given them every week three pieces of brass wire, each about nine inches long; and the theory was they were to buy their provisions with that currency in river-side villages. You can see how *that* worked. There were either no villages, or the people were hostile, or the director, who like the rest of us fed out of tins, with an occasional old he-goat thrown in, didn't want to stop the steamer for some more or less recondite reason. So, unless they swallowed the wire itself, or made loops of it to snare the fishes with, I don't see what good their extravagant salary could be to them. I must say it was paid with a regularity worthy of a large and honourable trading company. For the rest, the only thing to eat—though it didn't look eatable in the least—I saw in their possession was a few lumps of some stuff like half-cooked dough, of a dirty lavender colour, they kept wrapped in leaves, and now and then swallowed a piece of, but so small that it seemed done more for the looks of the thing than for any serious purpose of sustenance. Why in the name of all the gnawing devils of hunger they didn't go for us—they were thirty to five—and have a good tuck-in for once, amazes me now when I think of it. They were big powerful men, with not much capacity to weigh the consequences, with courage, with strength, even yet, though their skins were no longer glossy and their muscles no longer hard. And I saw that something restraining, one of those human secrets that baffle probability, had come into play there. I looked at them with a swift quickening of interest—not because it occurred to me I might be eaten by them before very long, though I own to you that just then I perceived—in a new light, as it were—how unwholesome the pilgrims looked, and I hoped, yes I positively hoped, that my aspect was not so—what shall I say? so —unappetizing: a touch of fantastic vanity which fitted well with the dream-sensation that pervaded all my days at that time. Perhaps I had a little fever, too. One can't live with one's finger exerlastingly on one's pulse. I had often 'a little fever,' or a little touch of other things—the playful paw-strokes of the wilderness, the preliminary trifling before the more serious onslaught which came in due course. Yes; I looked at them as you would on any human being, with a curiosity of their impulses, motives, capacities, weaknesses, when brought to the test of an inexorable physical necessity.

Restraint! What possible restraint? Was it superstition, disgust, patience, fear—or some kind of primitive honour? No fear can stand up to hunger, no patience can wear it out, disgust simply does not exist where hunger is; and as to superstition, beliefs, and what you may call principles, they are less than chaff in a breeze. Don't you know the devilry of lingering starvation, its exasperating torment, its black thoughts, its sombre and brooding ferocity? Well, I do. It takes a man all his inborn strength to fight hunger properly. It's really easier to face bereavement, dishonour, and the perdition of one's soul—than this kind of prolonged hunger. Sad, but true. And these chaps, too, had no earthly reason for any kind of scruple. Restraint! I would just as soon have expected restraint from a hyena prowling amongst the corpses of a battlefield. But there was the fact facing me—the fact dazzling, to be seen, like the foam on the depths of sea, like a ripple on an unfathomable enigma, a mystery greater—when I thought of it—than the curious, inexplicable note of desperate grief in this savage clamour that had swept by us on the riverbank, behind the blind whiteness of the fog.

"Two pilgrims were quarrelling in hurried whispers as to which bank. 'Left.' 'No, no; how can you? Right, right, of course.' 'It is very serious,' said the manager's voice behind me; 'I would be desolated if anything should happen to Mr. Kurtz before we came up.' I looked at him, and had not the slightest doubt he was sincere. He was just the kind of man who would wish to preserve appearances. That was his restraint. But when he muttered something about going on at once, I did not even take the trouble to answer him. I knew, and he knew, that it was impossible. Were we to let go our hold of the bottom, we would be absolutely in the air—in space. We wouldn't be able to tell where we were going to—whether up or down stream, or across —till we fetched against one bank or the other,—and then we wouldn't know at first which it was. Of course I made no move. I had no mind for a smash-up. You couldn't imagine a more deadly place for a shipwreck. Whether drowned at once or not, we were sure to perish speedily in one way or another. 'I authorize you to take all the risks,' he said, after a short silence. 'I refuse to take any,' I said shortly; which was just the answer he expected, though its tone might have surprised him. 'Well, I must defer to your judgment. You are captain,' he said, with marked civility. I turned my shoulder to him in sign of my appreciation, and looked into the fog. How long would it last? It was the most hopeless look-out. The approach to this Kurtz grubbing for ivory in the wretched bush was beset by as many dangers as though he had been an enchanted princess sleeping in a fabulous castle. 'Will they attack, do you think?' asked the manager, in a confidential tone.

"I did not think they would attack, for several obvious reasons. The thick fog was one. If they left the bank in their canoes they would get lost in it, as we would be if we attempted to move. Still, I had also judged the jungle of both banks quite impenetrable— and yet eyes were in it, eyes that had seen us. The riverside bushes were certainly very thick; but the undergrowth behind was evidently penetrable. However, during the short lift I had seen no canoes anywhere in the reach—certainly not abreast of the steamer. But what made the idea of attack inconceivable to me was the nature of the noise—of the cries we had heard. They had not the fierce character boding immediate hostile intention. Unexpected, wild, and violent as they had been, they had given me an irresistible impression of sorrow. The glimpse of the steamboat had for some reason filled those savages with unrestrained grief. The danger, if any, I expounded, was from our proximity to a great human passion let loose. Even extreme grief may ultimately vent itself in violence—but more generally takes the form of apathy. . . .

"You should have seen the pilgrims stare! They had no heart to grin, or even to revile me: but I believe they thought me gone mad—with fright, maybe. I delivered a regular lecture. My dear boys, it was no good bothering. Keep a look-out? Well, you may guess I watched the fog for the signs of lifting as a cat watches a mouse; but for anything else our eyes were of no more use to us than if we had been buried miles deep in a heap of cotton-wool. It felt like it, too—choking, warm, stifling. Besides, all I said, though it sounded extravagant, was absolutely true to fact. What we afterwards alluded to as an attack was really an attempt at repulse. The action was very far from being aggressive—it was not even defensive, in the usual sense: it was undertaken under the stress of desperation, and in its essence was purely protective.

"It developed itself, I should say, two hours after the fog lifted, and its commencement was at a spot, roughly speaking, about a mile and a half below Kurtz's station. We had just floundered and flopped round a bend, when I saw an islet, a mere grassy hummock of bright green, in the middle of the stream. It was the only thing of the kind; but as we opened the reach more, I perceived it was the head of a long sand-bank, or rather of a chain of shallow patches stretching down the middle of the river. They were discoloured, just awash, and the whole lot was seen just under the water, exactly as a man's backbone is seen running down the middle of his back under the skin. Now, as far as I did see, I could go to the right or to the left of this. I didn't know either channel, of course. The banks looked pretty well alike, the depth appeared the same; but as I had been informed the station was on the west side, I naturally headed for the western passage.

"No sooner had we fairly entered it than I became aware it was much narrower than I had supposed. To the left of us there was the long uninterrupted shoal, and to the right a high, steep bank heavily overgrown with bushes. Above the bush the trees stood in serried ranks. The twigs overhung the current thickly, and from distance to distance a large limb of some tree projected rigidly over the stream. It was then well on in the afternoon, the face of the forest was gloomy, and a broad strip of shadow had already fallen on the water. In this shadow we steamed up—very slowly, as you may imagine. I sheered her well inshore—the water being deepest near the bank, as the sounding-pole informed me.

"One of my hungry and forbearing friends was sounding in the bows just below me. This steamboat was exactly like a decked scow. On the deck, there were two little teak-wood houses, with doors and windows. The boiler was in the fore-end, and the machinery right astern. Over the whole there was a light roof, supported on stanchions. The funnel projected through that roof, and in front of the funnel a small cabin built of light planks served for a pilot-house. It contained a couch, two camp-stools, a loaded Martini-Henry leaning in one corner, a tiny table, and the steering-wheel. It had a wide door in front and a broad shutter at each side. All these were always thrown open, of course. I spent my days perched up there on the extreme fore-end of that roof, before the door. At night I slept, or tried to, on the couch. An athletic black belonging to some coast tribe, and educated by my poor predecessor, was the helmsman. He sported a pair of brass earrings, wore a blue cloth wrapper from the waist to the ankles, and thought all the world of himself. He was the most unstable kind of fool I had ever seen. He steered with no end of a swagger while you were by; but if he lost sight of you, he became instantly the prey of an abject funk, and would let that cripple of a steamboat get the upper hand of him in a minute.

"I was looking down at the sounding-pole, and feeling much annoyed to see at each try a little more of it stick out of that river, when I saw my poleman give up the business suddenly, and stretch himself flat on the deck, without even taking the trouble to haul his pole in. He kept hold on it though, and it trailed in the water. At the same time the fireman, whom I could also see below me, sat down abruptly before his furnace and ducked his head. I was amazed. Then I had to look at the river mighty quick, because there was a snag in the fairway. Sticks, little sticks, were flying about—thick: they were whizzing before my nose, dropping below me, striking behind me against my pilot-house. All this time the river, the shore, the woods, were very quiet—perfectly quiet. I could only hear the heavy splashing thump of the stern-wheel and the patter of these things. We cleared the snag clumsily.

Arrows, by Jove! We were being shot at! I stepped in quickly to close the shutter on the landside. That fool-helmsman, his hands on the spokes, was lifting his knees high, stamping his feet, champing his mouth, like a reined-in horse. Confound him! And we were staggering within ten feet of the bank. I had to lean right out to swing the heavy shutter, and I saw a face amongst the leaves on the level with my own, looking at me very fierce and steady; and then suddenly, as though a veil had been removed from my eyes, I made out, deep in the tangled gloom, naked breasts, arms, legs, glaring eyes,—the bush was swarming with human limbs in movement, glistening, of bronze colour. The twigs shook, swayed, and rustled, the arrows flew out of them, and then the shutter came to. 'Steer her straight,' I said to the helmsman. He held his head rigid, face forward; but his eyes rolled, he kept on lifting and setting down his feet gently, his mouth foamed a little. 'Keep quiet!' I said in a fury. I might just as well have ordered a tree not to sway in the wind. I darted out. Below me there was a great scuffle of feet on the iron deck; confused exclamations; a voice screamed, 'Can you turn back?' I caught sight of a V-shaped ripple on the water ahead. What? Another snag! A fusillade burst out under my feet. The pilgrims had opened with their Winchesters, and were simply squirting lead into that bush. A deuce of a lot of smoke came up and drove slowly forward. I swore at it. Now I couldn't see the ripple or the snag either. I stood in the doorway, peering, and the arrows came in swarms. They might have been poisoned, but they looked as though they wouldn't kill a cat. The bush began to howl. Our wood-cutters raised a warlike whoop; the report of a rifle just at my back deafened me. I glanced over my shoulder, and the pilot-house was yet full of noise and smoke when I made a dash at the wheel. The fool-nigger had dropped everything, to throw the shutter open and let off that Martini-Henry. He stood before the wide opening, glaring, and I yelled at him to come back, while I straightened the sudden twist out of that steamboat. There was no room to turn even if I had wanted to, the snag was somewhere very near ahead in that confounded smoke, there was no time to lose, so I just crowded her into the bank—right into the bank, where I knew the water was deep.

"We tore slowly along the overhanging bushes in a whirl of broken twigs and flying leaves. The fusillade below stopped short, as I had foreseen it would when the squirts got empty. I threw my head back to a glinting whizz that traversed the pilot-house, in at one shutter hole and out at the other. Looking past that mad helmsman, who was shaking the empty rifle and yelling at the shore, I saw vague forms of men running bent double, leaping, gliding, distinct, incomplete, evanescent. Something big appeared in the air before the shutter, the rifle went overboard, and the man stepped back swiftly, looked at me over his shoulder in an extraordinary, profound, familiar manner, and fell upon my feet. The side of his head hit the wheel twice, and the end of what appeared a long cane clattered round and knocked over a little camp-stool. It looked as though after wrenching that thing from somebody ashore he had lost his balance in the effort. The thin smoke had blown away, we were clear of the snag, and looking ahead I could see that in another hundred yards or so I would be free to sheer off, away from the bank; but my feet felt so very warm and wet that I had to look down. The man had rolled on his back and stared straight up at me; both his hands clutched that cane. It was the shaft of a spear that, either thrown or lunged through the opening, had caught him in the side just below the ribs; the blade had gone in out of sight, after making a frightful gash; my shoes were full; a pool of blood lay very still, gleaming dark-red under the wheel; his eyes shone with an amazing lustre. The fusillade burst out again. He looked at me anxiously, gripping the spear like something precious, with an air of being afraid I would try to take it away from him. I had to make an effort to free my eyes from his gaze and attend to the steering. With one hand I felt above my head for the line of the steam whistle, and jerked out screech after screech hurriedly. The tumult of angry and warlike yells was checked instantly, and then from the depths of the woods went out such a tremulous and prolonged wail of mournful fear and utter despair as may be imagined to follow the flight of the last hope from the earth. There was a great commotion in the bush; the shower of arrows stopped, a few dropping shots rang out sharply—then silence, in which the languid beat of the stern-wheel came plainly to my ears. I put the helm hard a-starboard at the moment when the pilgrim in pink pyjamas, very hot and agitated, appeared in the doorway. 'The manager sends me——' he began in an official tone, and stopped short. 'Good God!' he said, glaring at the wounded man.

"We two whites stood over him, and his lustrous and inquiring glance enveloped us both. I declare it looked as though he would presently put to us some question in an understandable language; but he died

without uttering a sound, without moving
out twitching a muscle. Only in the very l
as though in response to some sign we coul
some whisper we could not hear, he frowned heavily,
and that frown gave to his black death-mask an in-
conceivably sombre, brooding, and menacing expression. The lustre of inquiring glance faded swiftly into
vacant glassiness. 'Can you steer?' I asked the agent
eagerly. He looked very dubious; but I made a grab at
his arm, and he understood at once I meant him to
steer whether or no. To tell you the truth, I was mor-
bidly anxious to change my shoes and socks. 'He is
dead,' murmured the fellow, immensely impressed. 'No
doubt about it,' said I, tugging like mad at the shoe-
laces. 'And by the way, I suppose Mr. Kurtz is dead
as well by this time.'

"For the moment that was the dominant thought.
There was a sense of extreme disappointment, as
though I had found out I had been striving after something altogether without a substance. I couldn't have
been more disgusted if I had travelled all this way for
the sole purpose of talking with Mr. Kurtz. Talking
with . . . I flung one shoe overboard, and became aware
that was exactly what I had been looking forward to—
a talk with Kurtz. I made the strange discovery that I
had never imagined him as doing, you know, but as
discoursing. I didn't say to myself, 'Now I will never
see him,' or 'Now I will never shake him by the hand,'
but, 'now I will never hear him.' The man presented
himself as a voice. Not of course that I did not con-
nect him with some sort of action. Hadn't I been told
in all the tones of jealousy and admiration that he had
collected, bartered, swindled, or stolen more ivory than

the other agents together? That was not the point. The point was in his being a gifted creature, and that of all his gifts the one that stood out preëminently, that carried with it a sense of real presence, was his ability to talk, his words—the gift of expression, the bewildering, the illuminating, the most exalted and the most contemptible, the pulsating stream of light, or the deceitful flow from the heart of an impenetrable darkness.

"The other shoe went flying unto the devil-god of that river. I thought, By Jove! it's all over. We are too late; he has vanished—the gift has vanished, by means of some spear, arrow, or club. I will never hear that chap speak after all,—and my sorrow had a startling extravagance of emotion, even such as I had noticed in the howling sorrow of these savages in the bush. I couldn't have felt more of lonely desolation somehow, had I been robbed of a belief or had missed my destiny in life. . . . Why do you sigh in this beastly way, somebody? Absurd? Well, absurd. Good Lord! mustn't a man ever—— Here, give me some tobacco."...

There was a pause of profound stillness, then a match flared, and Marlow's lean face appeared, worn, hollow, with downward folds and dropped eyelids, with an aspect of concentrated attention; and as he took vigorous draws at his pipe, it seemed to retreat and advance out of the night in the regular flicker of the tiny flame. The match went out.

"Absurd!" he cried. "This is the worst of trying to tell. . . . Here you all are, each moored with two good addresses, like a hulk with two anchors, a butcher round one corner, a policeman round another, excellent appetites, and temperature normal—you hear—normal

from year's end to year's end. And you say, Absurd!
Absurd be—exploded! Absurd! My dear boys, what can
you expect from a man who out of sheer nervousness
had just flung overboard a pair of new shoes! Now I
think of it, it is amazing I did not shed tears. I am,
upon the whole, proud of my fortitude. I was cut to
the quick at the idea of having lost the inestimable
privilege of listening to the gifted Kurtz. Of course I
was wrong. The privilege was waiting for me. Oh, yes,
I heard more than enough. And I was right, too. A
voice. He was very little more than a voice. And I
heard—him—it—this voice—other voices—all of them
were so little more than voices—and the memory of
that time itself lingers around me, impalpable, like a
dying vibration of one immense jabber, silly, atrocious,
sordid, savage, or simply mean, without any kind of
sense. Voices, voices—even the girl herself—now——"

He was silent for a long time.

"I laid the ghost of his gifts at last with a lie," he
began, suddenly. "Girl! What? Did I mention a girl?
Oh, she is out of it—completely. They—the women I
mean—are out of it—should be out of it. We must help
them to stay in that beautiful world of their own, lest
ours gets worse. Oh, she had to be out of it. You should
have heard the disinterred body of Mr. Kurtz saying,
'My Intended.' You would have perceived directly then
how completely she was out of it. And the lofty frontal
bone of Mr. Kurtz! They say the hair goes on growing
sometimes, but this—ah—specimen, was impressively
bald. The wilderness had patted him on the head, and,
behold, it was like a ball—an ivory ball; it had caressed
him, and—lo!—he had withered; it had taken him,
loved him, embraced him, got into his veins, consumed

his flesh, and sealed his soul to its own by the inconceivable ceremonies of some devilish initiation. He was its spoiled and pampered favourite. Ivory? I should think so. Heaps of it, stacks of it. The old mud shanty was bursting with it. You would think there was not a single tusk left either above or below the ground in the whole country. 'Mostly fossil,' the manager had remarked, disparagingly. It was no more fossil than I am; but they call it fossil when it is dug up. It appears these niggers do bury the tusks sometimes—but evidently they couldn't bury this parcel deep enough to save the gifted Mr. Kurtz from his fate. We filled the steamboat with it, and had to pile a lot on the deck. Thus he could see and enjoy as long as he could see, because the appreciation of this favour had remained with him to the last. You should have heard him say, 'My ivory.' Oh yes, I heard him. 'My Intended, my ivory, my station, my river, my——' everything belonged to him. It made me hold my breath in expectation of hearing the wilderness burst into a prodigious peal of laughter that would shake the fixed stars in their places. Everything belonged to him—but that was a trifle. The thing was to know what he belonged to, how many powers of darkness claimed him for their own. That was the reflection that made you creepy all over. It was impossible—it was not good for one either—trying to imagine. He had taken a high seat amongst the devils of the land —I mean literally. You can't understand. How could you?—with solid pavement under your feet, surrounded by kind neighbours ready to cheer you or to fall on you, stepping delicately between the butcher and the policeman, in the holy terror of scandal and gallows and lunatic asylums—how can you imagine what particular

region of the first ages a man's untrammelled feet may
take him into by the way of solitude—utter solitude
without a policeman—by the way of silence—utter silence, where no warning voice of a kind neighbour can
be heard whispering of public opinion? These little
things make all the great difference. When they are
gone you must fall back upon your own innate strength,
upon your own capacity for faithfulness. Of course you
may be too much of a fool to go wrong—too dull even
to know you are being assaulted by the powers of darkness. I take it, no fool ever made a bargain for his soul
with the devil: the fool is too much of a fool, or the
devil too much of a devil—I don't know which. Or you
may be such a thunderingly exalted creature as to be
altogether deaf and blind to anything but heavenly
sights and sounds. Then the earth for you is only a
standing place—and whether to be like this is your loss
or your gain I won't pretend to say. But most of us are
neither one nor the other. The earth for us is a place
to live in, where we must put up with sights, with
sounds, with smells, too, by Jove!—breathe dead hippo,
so to speak, and not be contaminated. And there, don't
you see? your strength comes in, the faith in your ability for the digging of unostentatious holes to bury the
stuff in—your power of devotion, not to yourself, but to
an obscure, backbreaking business. And that's difficult
enough. Mind, I am not trying to excuse or even explain—I am trying to account to myself for—for—Mr.
Kurtz—for the shade of Mr. Kurtz. This initiated wraith
from the back of Nowhere honoured me with its amazing confidence before it vanished altogether. This was
because it could speak English to me. The original
Kurtz had been educated partly in England, and—as

he was good enough to say himself—his sympathies were in the right place. His mother was half-English, his father was half-French. All Europe contributed to the making of Kurtz; and by and by I learned that, most appropriately, the International Society for the Suppression of Savage Customs had intrusted him with the making of a report, for its future guidance. And he had written it, too. I've seen it, I've read it. It was eloquent, vibrating with eloquence, but too high-strung, I think. Seventeen pages of close writing he had found time for! But this must have been before his—let us say—nerves, went wrong, and caused him to preside at certain midnight dances ending with unspeakable rites, which—as far as I reluctantly gathered from what I heard at various times—were offered up to him—do you understand?—to Mr. Kurtz himself. But it was a beautiful piece of writing. The opening paragraph, however, in the light of later information, strikes me now as ominous. He began with the argument that we whites, from the point of development we had arrived at, 'must necessarily appear to them [savages] in the nature of supernatural beings—we approach them with the might as of a deity,' and so on, and so on. 'By the simple exercise of our will we can exert a power for good practically unbounded,' etc. etc. From that point he soared and took me with him. The peroration was magnificent, though difficult to remember, you know. It gave me the notion of an exotic Immensity ruled by an august Benevolence. It made me tingle with enthusiasm. This was the unbounded power of eloquence —of words—of burning noble words. There were no practical hints to interrupt the magic current of phrases, unless a kind of note at the foot of the last page, scrawled evidently much later, in an unsteady hand, may be regarded as the exposition of a method. It was very simple, and at the end of that moving appeal to every altruistic sentiment it blazed at you, luminous and terrifying, like a flash of lightning in a serene sky: 'Exterminate all the brutes!' The curious part was that he had apparently forgotten all about that valuable postscriptum, because, later on, when he in a sense came to himself, he repeatedly entreated me to take good care of 'my pamphlet' (he called it), as it was sure to have in the future a good influence upon his career. I had full information about all these things, and, besides, as it turned out, I was to have the care of his memory. I'd done enough for it to give me the indisputable right to lay it, if I choose, for an everlasting rest in the dust-bin of progress amongst all the sweepings and, figuratively speaking, all the dead cats of civilization. But then, you see, I can't choose. He won't be forgotten. Whatever he was, he was not common. He had the power to charm or frighten rudimentary souls into an aggravated witch-dance in his honour; he could also fill the small souls of the pilgrims with bitter misgivings: he had one devoted friend at least, and he had conquered one soul in the world that was neither rudimentary nor tainted with self-seeking. No; I can't forget him, though I am not prepared to affirm the fellow was exactly worth the life we lost in getting to him. I missed my late helmsman awfully,— I missed him even while his body was still lying in the pilot-house. Perhaps you will think it passing strange this regret for a savage who was no more account than a grain of sand in a black Sahara. Well, don't you see, he had done something, he had steered; for months I

had him at my back—a help—an instrument. It was a
kind of partnership. He steered for me—I had to look
after him, I worried about his deficiencies, and thus a
subtle bond had been created, of which I only became
aware when it was suddenly broken. And the intimate
profundity of that look he gave me when he received
his hurt remains to this day in my memory—like a claim
of distant kinship affirmed in a supreme moment.

"Poor fool! If he had only left that shutter alone. He
had no restraint, no restraint—just like Kurtz—a tree
swayed by the wind. As soon as I had put on a dry pair
of slippers, I dragged him out, after first jerking the
spear out of his side, which operation I confess I per-
formed with my eyes shut tight. His heels leaped together over the little door-step; his shoulders were
pressed to my breast; I hugged him from behind des-
perately. Oh! he was heavy, heavy; heavier than any
man on earth, I should imagine. Then without more
ado I tipped him overboard. The current snatched him
as though he had been a wisp of grass, and I saw the
body roll over twice before I lost sight of it for ever.
All the pilgrims and the manager were then congre-
gated on the awning-deck about the pilot-house, chattering at each other like a flock of excited magpies, and
there was a scandalized murmur at my heartless
promptitude. What they wanted to keep that body
hanging about for I can't guess. Embalm it, maybe. But
I had also heard another, and a very ominous, murmur
on the deck below. My friends the wood-cutters were
likewise scandalized, and with a better show of reason
—though I admit that the reason itself was quite inad-
missible. Oh, quite! I had made up my mind that if my
late helmsman was to be eaten, the fishes alone should

have him. He had been a very second-rate helmsman
while alive, but now he was dead he might have become a first-class temptation, and possibly cause some
startling trouble. Besides, I was anxious to take the
wheel, the man in pink pyjamas showing himself a
hopeless duffer at the business.

"This I did directly the simple funeral was over. We
were going half-speed, keeping right in the middle of
the stream, and I listened to the talk about me. They
had given up Kurtz, they had given up the station;
Kurtz was dead, and the station had been burnt—and
so on—and so on. The red-haired pilgrim was beside
himself with the thought that at least this poor Kurtz
had been properly avenged. 'Say! We must have made
a glorious slaughter of them in the bush. Eh? What do
you think? Say?' He positively danced, the blood-
thirsty little gingery beggar. And he had nearly fainted
when he saw the wounded man! I could not help saying, 'You made a glorious lot of smoke, anyhow.' I
had seen, from the way the tops of the bushes rustled
and flew, that almost all the shots had gone too high.
You can't hit anything unless you take aim and fire
from the shoulder; but these chaps fired from the hip
with their eyes shut. The retreat, I maintained—and I
was right—was caused by the screeching of the steam
whistle. Upon this they forgot Kurtz, and began to
howl at me with indignant protests.

"The manager stood by the wheel murmuring con-
fidentially about the necessity of getting well away
down the river before dark at all events, when I saw
in the distance a clearing on the riverside and the outlines of some sort of building. 'What's this?' I asked.

He clapped his hands in wonder. 'The station!' he cried. I edged in at once, still going half-speed.

"Through my glasses I saw the slope of a hill interspersed with rare trees and perfectly free from undergrowth. A long decaying building on the summit was half buried in the high grass; the large holes in the peaked roof gaped black from afar; the jungle and the woods made a background. There was no enclosure or fence of any kind; but there had been one apparently, for near the house half-a-dozen slim posts remained in a row, roughly trimmed, and with their upper ends ornamented with round carved balls. The rails, or whatever there had been between, had disappeared. Of course the forest surrounded all that. The river-bank was clear, and on the water-side I saw a white man under a hat like a cart-wheel beckoning persistently with his whole arm. Examining the edge of the forest above and below, I was almost certain I could see movements—human forms gliding here and there. I steamed past prudently, then stopped the engines and let her drift down. The man on the shore began to shout, urging us to land. 'We have been attacked,' screamed the manager. 'I know—I know. It's all right,' yelled back the other, as cheerful as you please. 'Come along. It's all right. I am glad.'

"His aspect reminded me of something I had seen—something funny I had seen somewhere. As I manœuvred to get alongside, I was asking myself, 'What does this fellow look like?' Suddenly I got it. He looked like a harlequin. His clothes had been made of some stuff that was brown holland probably, but it was covered with patches all over, with bright patches, blue, red, and yellow,—patches on the back, patches on the front, patches on elbows, on knees; coloured binding around his jacket, scarlet edging at the bottom of his trousers; and the sunshine made him look extremely gay and wonderfully neat withal, because you could see how beautifully all this patching had been done. A beardless, boyish face, very fair, no features to speak of, nose peeling, little blue eyes, smiles and frowns chasing each other over that open countenance like sunshine and shadow on a windswept plain. 'Look out, captain!' he cried; 'there's a snag lodged in here last night.' What! Another snag? I confess I swore shamefully. I had nearly holed my cripple, to finish off that charming trip. The harlequin on the bank turned his little pug-nose up to me. 'You English?' he asked, all smiles. 'Are you?' I shouted from the wheel. The smiles vanished, and he shook his head as if sorry for my disappointment. Then he brightened up. 'Never mind!' he cried, encouragingly. 'Are we in time?' I asked. 'He is up there,' he replied, with a toss of the head up the hill, and becoming gloomy all of a sudden. His face was like the autumn sky, overcast one moment and bright the next.

"When the manager, escorted by the pilgrims, all of them armed to the teeth, had gone to the house this chap came on board. 'I say, I don't like this. These natives are in the bush,' I said. He assured me earnestly it was all right. 'They are simple people,' he added; 'well, I am glad you came. It took me all my time to keep them off.' 'But you said it was all right,' I cried. 'Oh, they meant no harm,' he said; and as I stared he corrected himself, 'Not exactly.' Then vivaciously, 'My faith, your pilot-house wants a clean-up!' In the next breath he advised me to keep enough steam on the boiler to blow the whistle in case of any trouble. 'One good screech will do more for you than all your rifles. They are simple people,' he repeated. He rattled away at such a rate he quite overwhelmed me. He seemed to be trying to make up for lots of silence, and actually hinted, laughing, that such was the case. 'Don't you talk with Mr. Kurtz?' I said. 'You don't talk with that man—you listen to him,' he exclaimed with severe exaltation. 'But now——' He waved his arm, and in the twinkling of an eye was in the uttermost depths of despondency. In a moment he came up again with a jump, possessed himself of both my hands, shook them continuously, while he gabbled: 'Brother sailor . . . honour . . . pleasure . . . delight . . . introduce myself . . . Russian . . . son of an archpriest . . . Government of Tambov . . . What? Tobacco! English tobacco; the excellent English tobacco! Now, that's brotherly. Smoke? Where's a sailor that does not smoke?'

"The pipe soothed him, and gradually I made out he had run away from school, had gone to sea in a Russian ship; ran away again; served some time in English ships; was now reconciled with the archpriest. He made a point of that. 'But when one is young one must see things, gather experience, ideas; enlarge the mind.' 'Here!' I interrupted. 'You can never tell! Here I met Mr. Kurtz,' he said, youthfully solemn and reproachful. I held my tongue after that. It appears he had persuaded a Dutch trading-house on the coast to fit him out with stores and goods, and had started for the interior with a light heart, and no more idea of what would happen to him than a baby. He had been wandering about that river for nearly two years alone, cut off from everybody and everything. 'I am not so young as I look. I am twenty-five,' he said. 'At first old Van

Shuyten would tell me to go to the devil,' he narrated with keen enjoyment; 'but I stuck to him, and talked and talked, till at last he got afraid I would talk the hind-leg off his favourite dog, so he gave me some cheap things and a few guns, and told me he hoped he would never see my face again. Good old Dutchman, Van Shuyten. I've sent him one small lot of ivory a year ago, so that he can't call me a little thief when I get back. I hope he got it. And for the rest I don't care. I had some wood stacked for you. That was my old house. Did you see?'

"I gave him Towson's book. He made as though he would kiss me, but restrained himself. 'The only book I had left, and I thought I had lost it,' he said, looking at it ecstatically. 'So many accidents happen to a man going about alone, you know. Canoes get upset sometimes—and sometimes you've got to clear out so quick when the people get angry.' He thumbed the pages. 'You made notes in Russian?' I asked. He nodded. 'I thought they were written in cipher,' I said. He laughed, then became serious. 'I had lots of trouble to keep these people off,' he said. 'Did they want to kill you?' I asked. 'Oh, no!' he cried, and checked himself. 'Why did they attack us?' I pursued. He hesitated, then said shamefacedly. 'They don't want him to go.' 'Don't they?' I said, curiously. He nodded a nod full of mystery and wisdom. 'I tell you,' he cried, 'this man has enlarged my mind.' He opened his arms wide, staring at me with his little blue eyes that were perfectly round."

"I looked at him, lost in astonishment. There he was before me, in motley, as though he had absconded from a troupe of mimes, enthusiastic, fabulous. His very existence was improbable, inexplicable, and altogether bewildering. He was an insoluble problem. It was inconceivable how he had existed, how he had succeeded in getting so far, how he had managed to remain—why he did not instantly disappear. 'I went a little farther,' he said, 'then still a little farther—till I had gone so far that I don't know how I'll ever get back. Never mind. Plenty time. I can manage. You take Kurtz away quick —quick—I tell you.' The glamour of youth enveloped his parti-coloured rags, his destitution, his loneliness, the essential desolation of his futile wanderings. For months—for years—his life hadn't been worth a day's purchase; and there he was gallantly, thoughtlessly alive, to all appearance indestructible solely by the virtue of his few years and of his unreflecting audacity. I was seduced into something like admiration—like envy. Glamour urged him on, glamour kept him unscathed. He surely wanted nothing from the wilderness but space to breathe in and to push on through. His need was to exist, and to move onwards at the greatest possible risk, and with a maximum of privation. If the absolutely pure, uncalculating, unpractical spirit of adventure had ever ruled a human being, it ruled this be-patched youth. I almost envied him the possession of this modest and clear flame. It seemed to have consumed all thought of self so completely, that even while he was talking to you, you forgot that it was he—the man before your eyes—who had gone through these things. I did not envy him his devotion to Kurtz, though. He had not meditated over it. It came to him, and he accepted it with a sort of eager fatalism. I must say that to me it appeared about the most dangerous thing in every way he had come upon so far.

"They had come together unavoidably, like two ships becalmed near each other, and lay rubbing sides at last. I suppose Kurtz wanted an audience, because on a certain occasion, when encamped in the forest, they had talked all night, or more probably Kurtz had talked. 'We talked of everything,' he said, quite transported at the recollection. 'I forgot there was such a thing as sleep. The night did not seem to last an hour. Everything! Everything! . . . Of love, too.' 'Ah, he talked to you of love!' I said, much amused. 'It isn't what you think,' he cried, almost passionately. 'It was in general. He made me see things—things.'

"He threw his arms up. We were on deck at the time, and the headman of my wood-cutters, lounging near by, turned upon him his heavy and glittering eyes. I looked around, and I don't know why, but I assure you that never, never before, did this land, this river, this jungle, the very arch of this blazing sky, appear to me so hopeless and so dark, so impenetrable to human thought, so pitiless to human weakness. 'And, ever since, you have been with him, of course?' I said.

"On the contrary. It appears their intercourse had been very much broken by various causes. He had, as he informed me proudly, managed to nurse Kurtz through two illnesses (he alluded to it as you would to some risky feat), but as a rule Kurtz wandered alone, far in the depths of the forest. 'Very often coming to this station, I had to wait days and days before he would turn up,' he said. 'Ah, it was worth waiting for!—sometimes.' 'What was he doing? exploring or what?' I asked. 'Oh, yes, of course'; he had discovered lots of villages, a lake, too—he did not know exactly in what direction; it was dangerous to inquire too much —but mostly his expeditions had been for ivory. 'But he had no goods to trade with by that time,' I objected. 'There's a good lot of cartridges left even yet,' he answered, looking away. 'To speak plainly, he raided the country,' I said. He nodded. 'Not alone, surely!' He muttered something about the villages round that lake. 'Kurtz got the tribe to follow him, did he?' I suggested. He fidgeted a little. 'They adored him,' he said. The tone of these words was so extraordinary that I looked at him searchingly. It was curious to see his mingled eagerness and reluctance to speak of Kurtz. The man filled his life, occupied his thoughts, swayed his emotions. 'What can you expect?' he burst out; 'he came to them with thunder and lightning, you know—and they had never seen anything like it—and very terrible. He could be very terrible. You can't judge Mr. Kurtz as you would an ordinary man. No, no, no! Now—just to give you an idea—I don't mind telling you, he wanted to shoot me, too, one day—but I don't judge him.' 'Shoot you!' I cried. 'What for?' 'Well, I had a small lot of ivory the chief of that village near my house gave me. You see I used to shoot game for them. Well, he wanted it, and wouldn't hear reason. He declared he would shoot me unless I gave him the ivory and then cleared out of the country, because he could do so, and had a fancy for it, and there was nothing on earth to prevent him killing whom he jolly well pleased. And it was true, too. I gave him the ivory. What did I care! But I didn't clear out. No, no. I couldn't leave him. I had to be careful, of course, till we got friendly again for a time. He had his second illness then. Afterwards I had to keep out of the way; but I didn't mind. He was living for the most part in those villages on the lake. When he came down to the river, sometimes he would take to me, and sometimes it was better for me to be careful. This man suffered too much. He hated all this, and somehow he couldn't get away. When I had a chance I begged him to try and leave while there was time; I offered to go back with him. And he would say yes, and then he would remain; go off on another ivory hunt; disappear for weeks; forget himself amongst these people—forget himself—you know.' 'Why! he's mad,' I said. He protested indignantly. Mr. Kurtz couldn't be mad. If I had heard him talk, only two days ago, I wouldn't dare hint at such a thing. . . . I had taken up my binoculars while we talked, and was looking at the shore, sweeping the limit of the forest at each side and at the back of the house. The consciousness of there being people in that bush, so silent, so quiet—as silent and quiet as the ruined house on the hill—made me uneasy. There was no sign on the face of nature of this amazing tale that was not so much told as suggested to me in desolate exclamations, completed by shrugs, in interrupted phrases, in hints ending in deep sighs. The woods were unmoved, like a mask—heavy, like the closed door of a prison—they looked with their air of hidden knowledge, of patient expectation, of unapproachable silence. The Russian was explaining to me that it was only lately that Mr. Kurtz had come down to the river, bringing along with him all the fighting men of that lake tribe. He had been absent for several months—getting himself adored, I suppose—and had come down unexpectedly, with the intention to all appearance of making a raid either across the river or down stream. Evidently the appetite for more ivory had got the better of the—what shall I say?—less material aspirations. However he had got much worse suddenly. 'I heard he was lying helpless, and so I came up—took my chance,' said the Russian. 'Oh, he is bad, very bad.' I directed my glass to the house. There were no signs of life, but there was the ruined roof, the long mud wall peeping above the grass, with three little square window-holes, no two of the same size; all this brought within reach of my hand, as it were. And then I made a brusque movement, and one of the remaining posts of that vanished fence leaped up in the field of

my glass. You remember I told you I had been struck
at the distance by certain attempts at ornamentation,
rather remarkable in the ruinous aspect of the place.
Now I had suddenly a nearer view, and its first result
was to make me throw my head back as if before a
blow. Then I went carefully from post to post with my
glass, and I saw my mistake. These round knobs were
not ornamental but symbolic; they were expressive and
puzzling, striking and disturbing—food for thought and
also for vultures if there had been any looking down
from the sky; but at all events for such ants as were
industrious enough to ascend the pole. They would
have been even more impressive, those heads on the
stakes, if their faces had not been turned to the house.
Only one, the first I had made out, was facing my way.
I was not so shocked as you may think. The start back
I had given was really nothing but a movement of surprise. I had expected to see a knob of wood there, you
know. I returned deliberately to the first I had seen—
and there it was, black, dried, sunken, with closed eyelids,—a head that seemed to sleep at the top of that
pole, and with the shrunken dry lips showing a narrow
white line of the teeth, was smiling, too, smiling continuously at some endless and jocose dream of that
eternal slumber.

"I am not disclosing any trade secrets. In fact, the
manager said afterwards that Mr. Kurtz's methods had
ruined the district. I have no opinion on that point,
but I want you clearly to understand that there was
nothing exactly profitable in these heads being there.
They only showed that Mr. Kurtz lacked restraint in
the gratification of his various lusts, that there was
something wanting in him—some small matter which,

when the pressing need arose, could not be found under his magnificent eloquence. Whether he knew of this deficiency himself I can't say. I think the knowledge came to him at last—only at the very last. But the wilderness had found him out early, and had taken on him a terrible vengeance for the fantastic invasion. I think it had whispered to him things about himself which he did not know, things of which he had no conception till he took counsel with this great solitude —and the whisper had proved irresistibly fascinating. It echoed loudly within him because he was hollow at the core. . . . I put down the glass, and the head that had appeared near enough to be spoken to seemed at once to have leaped away from me into inaccessible distance.

"The admirer of Mr. Kurtz was a bit crestfallen. In a hurried, indistinct voice he began to assure me he had not dared to take these—say, symbols—down. He was not afraid of the natives; they would not stir till Mr. Kurtz gave the word. His ascendancy was extraordinary. The camps of these people surrounded the place, and the chiefs came every day to see him. They would crawl. . . . 'I don't want to know anything of the ceremonies used when approaching Mr. Kurtz,' I shouted. Curious, this feeling that came over me that such details would be more intolerable than those heads drying on the stakes under Mr. Kurtz's windows. After all, that was only a savage sight, while I seemed at one bound to have been transported into some lightless region of subtle horrors, where pure, uncomplicated savagery was a positive relief, being something that had a right to exist—obviously—in the sunshine. The young man looked at me with surprise. I suppose it did not

occur to him that Mr. Kurtz was no idol
forgot I hadn't heard any of these splendid
on, what was it? on love, justice, conduc
what not. If it had come to crawling before Mr. Kurtz,
he crawled as much as the veriest savage of them all.
I had no idea of the conditions, he said: these heads
were the heads of rebels. I shocked him excessively by
laughing. Rebels! What would be the next definition I
was to hear? There had been enemies, criminals, workers—and these were rebels. Those rebellious heads
looked very subdued to me on their sticks. 'You don't
know how such a life tries a man like Kurtz,' cried
Kurtz's last disciple. 'Well, and you?' I said. 'I! I! I am
a simple man. I have no great thoughts. I want nothing
from anybody. How can you compare me to . . . ?' His
feelings were too much for speech, and suddenly he
broke down. 'I don't understand,' he groaned. 'I've been
doing my best to keep him alive, and that's enough. I
had no hand in all this. I have no abilities. There hasn't
been a drop of medicine or a mouthful of invalid food
for months here. He was shamefully abandoned. A man
like this, with such ideas. Shamefully! Shamefully! I—
I—haven't slept for the last ten nights. . . .'

"His voice lost itself in the calm of the evening. The
long shadows of the forest had slipped down hill while
we talked, had gone far beyond the ruined hovel, beyond the symbolic row of stakes. All this was in the
gloom, while we down there were yet in the sunshine,
and the stretch of the river abreast of the clearing
glittered in a still and dazzling splendour, with a
murky and overshadowed bend above and below. Not
a living soul was seen on the shore. The bushes did not
rustle.

"Suddenly round the corner of the house a group of men appeared, as though they had come up from the ground. They waded waist-deep in the grass, in a compact body, bearing an improvised stretcher in their midst. Instantly, in the emptiness of the landscape, a cry arose whose shrillness pierced the still air like a sharp arrow flying straight to the very heart of the land; and, as if by enchantment, streams of human beings—of naked human beings—with spears in their hands, with bows, with shields, with wild glances and savage movements, were poured into the clearing by the dark-faced and pensive forest. The bushes shook, the grass swayed for a time, and then everything stood still in attentive immobility.

" 'Now, if he does not say the right thing to them we are all done for,' said the Russian at my elbow. The knot of men with the stretcher had stopped, too, halfway to the steamer, as if petrified. I saw the man on the stretcher sit up, lank and with an uplifted arm, above the shoulders of the bearers. 'Let us hope that the man who can talk so well of love in general will find some particular reason to spare us this time,' I said. I resented bitterly the absurd danger of our situation, as if to be at the mercy of that atrocious phantom had been a dishonouring necessity. I could not hear a sound, but through my glasses I saw the thin arm extended commandingly, the lower jaw moving, the eyes of that apparition shining darkly far in its bony head that nodded with grotesque jerks. Kurtz—Kurtz—that means short in German—don't it? Well, the name was as true as everything else in his life—and death. He looked at least seven feet long. His covering had fallen off, and his body emerged from it pitiful and appalling as from a winding-sheet. I could see the cage of his ribs all astir, the bones of his arm waving. It was as though an animated image of death carved out of old ivory had been shaking its hand with menaces at a motionless crowd of men made of dark and glittering bronze. I saw him open his mouth wide—it gave him a weirdly voracious aspect, as though he had wanted to swallow all the air, all the earth, all the men before him. A deep voice reached me faintly. He must have been shouting. He fell back suddenly. The stretcher shook as the bearers staggered forward again, and almost at the same time I noticed that the crowd of savages was vanishing without any perceptible movements of retreat, as if the forest that had ejected these beings so suddenly had drawn them in again as the breath is drawn in a long aspiration.

"Some of the pilgrims behind the stretcher carried his arms—two shot-guns, a heavy rifle, and a light revolver-carbine—the thunderbolts of that pitiful Jupiter. The manager bent over him murmuring as he walked beside his head. They laid him down in one of the little cabins—just a room for a bedplace and a camp-stool or two, you know. We had brought his belated correspondence, and a lot of torn envelopes and open letters littered his bed. His hand roamed feebly amongst these papers. I was struck by the fire of his eyes and the composed languor of his expression. It was not so much the exhaustion of disease. He did not seem in pain. This shadow looked satiated and calm, as though for the moment it had had its fill of all the emotions.

"He rustled one of the letters, and looking straight in my face said, 'I am glad.' Somebody had been writing to him about me. These special recommendations

were turning up again. The volume of tone he emitted
without effort, almost without the trouble of moving
his lips, amazed me. A voice! A voice! It was grave,
profound, vibrating, while the man did not seem capable of a whisper. However, he had enough strength
in him—factitious no doubt—to very nearly make an
end of us, as you shall hear directly.

"The manager appeared silently in the doorway; I
stepped out at once and he drew the curtain after me.
The Russian, eyed curiously by the pilgrims, was staring at the shore. I followed the direction of his glance.

"Dark human shapes could be made out in the distance, flitting indistinctly against the gloomy border of
the forest, and near the river two bronze figures, leaning on tall spears, stood in the sunlight under fantastic
headdresses of spotted skins, warlike and still in statu-
esque repose. And from right to left along the lighted
shore moved a wild and gorgeous apparition of a
woman.

"She walked with measured steps, draped in striped
and fringed cloths, treading the earth proudly, with a
slight jingle and flash of barbarous ornaments. She carried her head high; her hair was done in the shape of a
helmet; she had brass leggings to the knee, brass wire
gauntlets to the elbow, a crimson spot on her tawny
cheek, innumerable necklaces of glass beads on her
neck; bizarre things, charms, gifts of witch-men, that
hung about her, glittered and trembled at every step.
She must have had the value of several elephant tusks
upon her. She was savage and superb, wild-eyed and
magnificent; there was something ominous and stately
in her deliberate progress. And in the hush that had
fallen suddenly upon the whole sorrowful land, the

immense wilderness, the colossal body of the fecund
and mysterious life seemed to look at the image of its
own tenebrous and passionate soul.

"She came abreast of the steamer, stood still, and
faced us. Her long shadow fell to the water's edge. Her
face had a tragic and fierce aspect of wild sorrow and
dumb pain mingled with the fear of some struggling,
half-shaped resolve. She stood looking at us without a
stir, and like the wilderness itself, with an air of brooding over an inscrutable purpose. A whole minute
passed, and then she made a step forward. There was
a low jingle, a glint of yellow metal, a sway of fringed
draperies, and she stopped as if her heart had failed
her. The young fellow by my side growled. The pilgrims murmured at my back. She looked at us all as
if her life had depended upon the unswerving steadi-
ness of her glance. Suddenly she opened her bared
arms and threw them up rigid above her head, as
though in an uncontrollable desire to touch the sky,
and at the same time the swift shadows darted out on
the earth, swept around on the river, gathering the
steamer into a shadowy embrace. A formidable silence
hung over the scene.

"She turned away slowly, walked on, following the
bank, and passed into the bushes to the left. Once only
her eyes gleamed back at us in the dusk of the thickets
before she disappeared.

" 'If she had offered to come aboard I really think I
would have tried to shoot her,' said the man of patches,
nervously. 'I have been risking my life every day for the
last fortnight to keep her out of the house. She got in
one day and kicked up a row about those miserable
rags I picked up in the storeroom to mend my clothes

with. I wasn't decent. At least it must have been that, for she talked like a fury to Kurtz for an hour, pointing at me now and then. I don't understand the dialect of this tribe. Luckily for me, I fancy Kurtz felt too ill that day to care, or there would have been mischief. I don't understand. . . . No—it's too much for me. Ah, well, it's all over now.'

"At this moment I heard Kurtz's deep voice behind the curtain: 'Save me!—save the ivory, you mean. Don't tell me. Save *me!* Why, I've had to save you. You are interrupting my plans now. Sick! Sick! Not so sick as you would like to believe. Never mind. I'll carry my ideas out yet—I will return. I'll show you what can be done. You with your little peddling notions—you are interfering with me. I will return. I. . . .'

"The manager came out. He did me the honour to take me under the arm and lead me aside. 'He is very low, very low,' he said. He considered it necessary to sigh, but neglected to be consistently sorrowful. 'We have done all we could for him—haven't we? But there is no disguising the fact, Mr. Kurtz has done more harm than good to the Company. He did not see the time was not ripe for vigorous action. Cautiously, cautiously—that's my principle. We must be cautious yet. The district is closed to us for a time. Deplorable! Upon the whole, the trade will suffer. I don't deny there is a remarkable quantity of ivory—mostly fossil. We must save it, at all events—but look how precarious the position is—and why? Because the method is unsound.' 'Do you,' said I, looking at the shore, 'call it "unsound method"?' 'Without doubt,' he exclaimed hotly. 'Don't you?' . . .

" 'No method at all,' I murmured after a while. 'Exactly,' he exulted. 'I anticipated this. Shows a complete want of judgment. It is my duty to point it out in the proper quarter.' 'Oh,' said I, 'that fellow—what's his name?—the brickmaker, will make a readable report for you.' He appeared confounded for a moment. It seemed to me I had never breathed an atmosphere so vile, and I turned mentally to Kurtz for relief—positively for relief. 'Nevertheless I think Mr. Kurtz is a remarkable man,' I said with emphasis. He started, dropped on me a cold heavy glance, said very quietly, 'he *was*,' and turned his back on me. My hour of favour was over; I found myself lumped along with Kurtz as a partisan of methods for which the time was not ripe: I was unsound! Ah! but it was something to have at least a choice of nightmares.

"I had turned to the wilderness really, not to Mr. Kurtz, who, I was ready to admit, was as good as buried. And for a moment it seemed to me as if I also were buried in a vast grave full of unspeakable secrets. I felt an intolerable weight oppressing my breast, the smell of the damp earth, the unseen presence of victorious corruption, the darkness of an impenetrable night. . . . The Russian tapped me on the shoulder. I heard him mumbling and stammering something about 'brother seaman—couldn't conceal—knowledge of matters that would affect Mr. Kurtz's reputation.' I waited. For him evidently Mr. Kurtz was not in his grave; I suspect that for him Mr. Kurtz was one of the immortals. 'Well!' said I at last, 'speak out. As it happens, I am Mr. Kurtz's friend—in a way.'

"He stated with a good deal of formality that had we not been 'of the same profession,' he would have kept the matter to himself without regard to consequences.

'He suspected there was an active ill will towards him on the part of these white men that——' 'You are right,' I said, remembering a certain conversation I had overheard. 'The manager thinks you ought to be hanged.' He showed a concern at this intelligence which amused me at first. 'I had better get out of the way quietly,' he said, earnestly. 'I can do no more for Kurtz now, and they would soon find some excuse. What's to stop them? There's a military post three hundred miles from here.' 'Well, upon my word,' said I, 'perhaps you had better go if you have any friends amongst the savages near by.' 'Plenty,' he said. 'They are simple people—and I want nothing, you know.' He stood biting his lip, then: 'I don't want any harm to happen to these whites here, but of course I was thinking of Mr. Kurtz's reputation —but you are a brother seaman and——' 'All right,' said I, after a time. 'Mr. Kurtz's reputation is safe with me.' I did not know how truly I spoke.

"He informed me, lowering his voice, that it was Kurtz who had ordered the attack to be made on the steamer. 'He hated sometimes the idea of being taken away—and then again. . . . But I don't understand these matters. I am a simple man. He thought it would scare you away—that you would give it up, thinking him dead. I could not stop him. Oh, I had an awful time of it this last month.' 'Very well,' I said. 'He is all right now.' 'Ye-e-es,' he muttered, not very convinced apparently. 'Thanks,' said I; 'I shall keep my eyes open.' 'But quiet—eh?' he urged, anxiously. 'It would be awful for his reputation if anybody here——' I promised a complete discretion with great gravity. 'I have a canoe and three black fellows waiting not very far. I am off. Could you give me a few Martini-Henry cartridges?' I could, and did, with proper secrecy. He helped himself, with a wink to me, to a handful of my tobacco. 'Between sailors—you know—good English tobacco.' At the door of the pilot-house he turned round—'I say, haven't you a pair of shoes you could spare?' He raised one leg. 'Look.' The soles were tied with knotted strings sandal-wise under his bare feet. I rooted out an old pair, at which he looked with admiration before tucking it under his left arm. One of his pockets (bright red) was bulging with cartridges, from the other (dark blue) peeped 'Towson's Inquiry,' etc., etc. He seemed to think himself excellently well equipped for a renewed encounter with the wilderness. 'Ah! I'll never, never meet such a man again. You ought to have heard him recite poetry—his own, too, it was, he told me. Poetry!' He rolled his eyes at the recollection of these delights. 'Oh, he enlarged my mind!' 'Good-bye,' said I. He shook hands and vanished in the night. Sometimes I ask myself whether I had ever really seen him—whether it was possible to meet such a phenomenon! . . .

"When I woke up shortly after midnight his warning came to my mind with its hint of danger that seemed, in the starred darkness, real enough to make me get up for the purpose of having a look round. On the hill a big fire burned, illuminating fitfully a crooked corner of the station-house. One of the agents with a picket of a few of our blacks, armed for the purpose, was keeping guard over the ivory; but deep within the forest, red gleams that wavered, that seemed to sink and rise from the ground amongst confused columnar shapes of intense blackness, showed the exact position of the camp where Mr. Kurtz's adorers were keeping their uneasy vigil. The monotonous beating of a big drum filled the air with muffled shocks and a lingering vibration. A steady droning sound of many men chanting each to himself some weird incantation came out from the black, flat wall of the woods as the humming of bees comes out of a hive, and had a strange narcotic effect upon my half-awake senses. I believe I dozed off leaning over the rail, till an abrupt burst of yells, an overwhelming outbreak of a pent-up and mysterious frenzy, woke me up in a bewildered wonder. It was cut short all at once, and the low droning went on with an effect of audible and soothing silence. I glanced casually into the little cabin. A light was burning within, but Mr. Kurtz was not there.

"I think I would have raised an outcry if I had believed my eyes. But I didn't believe them at first—the thing seemed so impossible. The fact is I was completely unnerved by a sheer blank fright, pure abstract terror, unconnected with any distinct shape of physical danger. What made this emotion so overpowering was —how shall I define it?—the moral shock I received, as if something altogether monstrous, intolerable to thought and odious to the soul, had been thrust upon me unexpectedly. This lasted of course the merest fraction of a second, and then the usual sense of commonplace, deadly danger, the possibility of a sudden onslaught and massacre, or something of the kind, which I saw impending, was positively welcome and composing. It pacified me, in fact, so much, that I did not raise an alarm.

"There was an agent buttoned up inside an ulster and sleeping on a chair within three feet of me. The yells had not awakened him; he snored very slightly; I left him to his slumbers and leaped ashore. I did not betray Mr. Kurtz—it was ordered I should never betray him—it was written I should be loyal to the nightmare of my choice. I was anxious to deal with this shadow by myself alone,—and to this day I don't know why I was so jealous of sharing with any one the peculiar blackness of that experience.

"As soon as I got on the bank I saw a trail—a broad trail through the grass. I remember the exaltation with which I said to myself, 'He can't walk—he is crawling on all-fours—I've got him.' The grass was wet with dew. I strode rapidly with clenched fists. I fancy I had some vague notion of falling upon him and giving him a drubbing. I don't know. I had some imbecile thoughts. The knitting old woman with the cat obtruded herself upon my memory as a most improper person to be sitting at the other end of such an affair. I saw a row of pilgrims squirting lead in the air out of Winchesters held to the hip. I thought I would never get back to the steamer, and imagined myself living alone and unarmed in the woods to an advanced age. Such silly things—you know. And I remember I confounded the beat of the drum with the beating of my heart, and was pleased at its calm regularity.

"I kept to the track though—then stopped to listen. The night was very clear; a dark blue space, sparkling with dew and starlight, in which black things stood very still. I thought I could see a kind of motion ahead of me. I was strangely cocksure of everything that night. I actually left the track and ran in a wide semicircle (I verily believe chuckling to myself) so as to get in front of that stir, of that motion I had seen—if indeed I had seen anything. I was circumventing Kurtz as though it had been a boyish game.

"I came upon him, and, if he had not heard me coming, I would have fallen over him, too, but he got up in time. He rose, unsteady, long, pale, indistinct, like a vapour exhaled by the earth, and swayed slightly, misty and silent before me; while at my back the fires loomed between the trees, and the murmur of many voices issued from the forest. I had cut him off cleverly; but when actually confronting him I seemed to come to my senses, I saw the danger in its right proportion. It was by no means over yet. Suppose he began to shout? Though he could hardly stand, there was still plenty of vigour in his voice. 'Go away—hide yourself,' he said, in that profound tone. It was very awful. I glanced back. We were within thirty yards from the nearest fire. A black figure stood up, strode on long black legs, waving long black arms, across the glow. It had horns—antelope horns, I think—on its head. Some sorcerer, some witch-man, no doubt; it looked fiendlike enough. 'Do you know what you are doing?' I whispered. 'Perfectly,' he answered, raising his voice for that single word: it sounded to me far off and yet loud, like a hail through a speaking-trumpet. If he makes a row we are lost, I thought to myself. This clearly was not a case for fisticuffs, even apart from the very natural aversion I had to beat that Shadow—this wandering and tormented thing. 'You will be lost,' I said—'utterly lost.' One gets sometimes such a flash of inspiration, you know. I did say the right thing, though indeed he could not have been more irretrievably lost than he was at this very moment, when the foundations of our intimacy were being laid—to endure—to endure—even to the end—even beyond.

"'I had immense plans,' he muttered irresolutely. 'Yes,' said I; 'but if you try to shout I'll smash your head with——' There was not a stick or a stone near. 'I will throttle you for good,' I corrected myself. 'I was on the threshold of great things,' he pleaded, in a voice of longing, with a wistfulness of tone that made my blood run cold. 'And now for this stupid scoundrel——' 'Your success in Europe is assured in any case,' I affirmed, steadily. I did not want to have the throttling of him, you understand—and indeed it would have been very little use for any practical purpose. I tried to break the spell—the heavy, mute spell of the wilderness—that seemed to draw him to its pitiless breast by the awakening of forgotten and brutal instincts, by the memory of gratified and monstrous passions. This alone, I was convinced, had driven him out to the edge of the forest, to the bush, towards the gleam of fires, the throb of drums, the drone of weird incantations; this alone had beguiled his unlawful soul beyond the bounds of permitted aspirations. And, don't you see, the terror of the position was not in being knocked on the head—though I had a very lively sense of that danger, too—but in this, that I had to deal with a being to whom I could not appeal in the name of anything high or low. I had, even like the niggers, to invoke him—himself—his own exalted and incredible degradation. There was nothing either above or below him, and I knew it. He had kicked himself loose of the earth. Confound the man! he had kicked the very earth to pieces. He was alone, and I before him did not know whether I stood on the ground or floated in the air. I've been telling you what we said—repeating the phrases we pronounced—but what's the good? They were common everyday words—the familiar, vague sounds exchanged on every waking day of life. But what of that? They had behind them, to my mind, the terrific suggestiveness of words heard in dreams, of phrases spoken in nightmares. Soul! If anybody had ever struggled with a soul, I am the man. And I wasn't arguing with a lunatic either. Believe me or not, his intelligence was perfectly clear—concentrated, it is true, upon himself with horrible intensity, yet clear; and therein was my only chance—barring, of course, the killing him there and then, which wasn't so good, on account of unavoidable noise. But his soul was mad. Being alone in the wilderness, it had looked within itself, and, by heavens! I tell you, it had gone mad. I had—for my sins, I suppose—to go through the ordeal of looking into it myself. No eloquence could have been so withering to one's belief in mankind as his final burst of sincerity. He struggled with himself, too. I saw it,—I heard it. I saw the inconceivable mystery of a soul that knew no restraint, no faith, and no fear, yet struggling blindly with itself. I kept my head pretty well; but when I had him at last stretched on the couch, I wiped my forehead, while my legs shook under me as though I had carried half a ton on my back down that hill. And yet I had only supported him, his bony arm clasped round my neck—and he was not much heavier than a child.

"When next day we left at noon, the crowd, of whose presence behind the curtain of trees I had been acutely conscious all the time, flowed out of the woods again, filled the clearing, covered the slope with a mass of naked, breathing, quivering, bronze bodies. I steamed up a bit, then swung downstream, and two thousand

eyes followed the evolutions of the splashing, thump-
ing, fierce river-demon beating the water with its terrible tail and breathing black smoke into the air. In front
of the first rank, along the river, three men, plastered
with bright red earth from head to foot, strutted to and
fro restlessly. When we came abreast again, they faced
the river, stamped their feet, nodded their horned
heads, swayed their scarlet bodies; they shook towards
the fierce river-demon a bunch of black feathers, a
mangy skin with a pendent tail—something that looked
like a dried gourd; they shouted periodically together
strings of amazing words that resembled no sounds of
human language; and the deep murmurs of the crowd,
interrupted suddenly, were like the responses of some
satanic litany.

"We had carried Kurtz into the pilot-house: there
was more air there. Lying on the couch, he stared
through the open shutter. There was an eddy in the
mass of human bodies, and the woman with helmeted
head and tawny cheeks rushed out to the very brink of
the stream. She put out her hands, shouted something,
and all that wild mob took up the shout in a roaring
chorus of articulated, rapid, breathless utterance.

" 'Do you understand this?' I asked.

"He kept on looking out past me with fiery, longing
eyes, with a mingled expression of wistfulness and hate.
He made no answer, but I saw a smile, a smile of indefinable meaning, appear on his colourless lips that a
moment after twitched convulsively. 'Do I not?' he said
slowly, gasping, as if the words had been torn out of
him by a supernatural power.

"I pulled the string of the whistle, and I did this because I saw the pilgrims on deck getting out their rifles

with an air of anticipating a jolly lark. At the sudden screech there was a movement of abject terror through that wedged mass of bodies. 'Don't! don't you frighten them away,' cried someone on deck disconsolately. I pulled the string time after time. They broke and ran, they leaped, they crouched, they swerved, they dodged the flying terror of the sound. The three red chaps had fallen flat, face down on the shore, as though they had been shot dead. Only the barbarous and superb woman did not so much as flinch, and stretched tragically her bare arms after us over the sombre and glittering river.

"And then that imbecile crowd down on the deck started their little fun, and I could see nothing more for smoke.

"The brown current ran swiftly out of the heart of darkness, bearing us down towards the sea with twice the speed of our upward progress; and Kurtz's life was running swiftly, too, ebbing, ebbing out of his heart into the sea of inexorable time. The manager was very placid, he had no vital anxieties now, he took us both in with a comprehensive and satisfied glance: the 'affair' had come off as well as could be wished. I saw the time approaching when I would be left alone of the party of 'unsound method.' The pilgrims looked upon me with disfavour. I was, so to speak, numbered with the dead. It is strange how I accepted this unforeseen partnership, this choice of nightmares forced upon me in the tenebrous land invaded by these mean and greedy phantoms.

"Kurtz discoursed. A voice! a voice! It rang deep to the very last. It survived his strength to hide in the

magnificent folds of eloquence the barren darkness of
his heart. Oh, he struggled! he struggled! The wastes of
his weary brain were haunted by shadowy images now
—images of wealth and fame revolving obsequiously
round his unextinguishable gift of noble and lofty expression. My Intended, my station, my career, my ideas
—these were the subjects for the occasional utterances
of elevated sentiments. The shade of the original Kurtz
frequented the bedside of the hollow sham, whose fate
it was to be buried presently in the mould of primeval
earth. But both the diabolic love and the unearthly
hate of the mysteries it had penetrated fought for the
possession of that soul satiated with primitive emotions,
avid of lying fame, or sham distinction, of all the appearances of success and power.

"Sometimes he was contemptibly childish. He de-
sired to have kings meet him at railway-stations on his
return from some ghastly Nowhere, where he intended
to accomplish great things. 'You show them you have
in you something that is really profitable, and then
there will be no limits to the recognition of your ability,' he would say. 'Of course you must take care of the
motives—right motives—always.' The long reaches that
were like one and the same reach, monotonous bends
that were exactly alike, slipped past the steamer with
their multitude of secular trees looking patiently after
this grimy fragment of another world, the forerunner
of change, of conquest, of trade, of massacres, of bless-
ings. I looked ahead—piloting. 'Close the shutter,' said
Kurtz suddenly one day; 'I can't bear to look at this.' I
did so. There was a silence. 'Oh, but I will wring your
heart yet!' he cried at the invisible wilderness.

"We broke down—as I had expected—and had to lie

up for repairs at the head of an island. This delay was the first thing that shook Kurtz's confidence. One morning he gave me a packet of papers and a photograph—the lot tied together with a shoe-string. 'Keep this for me,' he said. 'This noxious fool' (meaning the manager) 'is capable of prying into my boxes when I am not looking.' In the afternoon I saw him. He was lying on his back with closed eyes, and I withdrew quietly, but I heard him mutter, 'Live rightly, die, die . . .' I listened. There was nothing more. Was he rehearsing some speech in his sleep, or was it a fragment of a phrase from some newspaper article? He had been writing for the papers and meant to do so again, 'for the furthering of my ideas. It's a duty.'

"His was an impenetrable darkness. I looked at him as you peer down at a man who is lying at the bottom of a precipice where the sun never shines. But I had not much time to give him, because I was helping the engine-driver to take to pieces the leaky cylinders, to straighten a bent connecting-rod, and in other such matters. I lived in an infernal mess of rust, filings, nuts, bolts, spanners, hammers, ratchet-drills—things I abominate, because I don't get on with them. I tended the little forge we fortunately had aboard; I toiled wearily in a wretched scrap-heap—unless I had the shakes too bad to stand.

"One evening coming in with a candle I was startled to hear him say a little tremulously, 'I am lying here in the dark waiting for death.' The light was within a foot of his eyes. I forced myself to murmur, 'Oh, nonsense!' and stood over him as if transfixed.

"Anything approaching the change that came over his features I have never seen before, and hope never

to see again. Oh, I wasn't touched. I was fa
was as though a veil had been rent. I saw oi
face the expression of sombre pride, of ruth... power,
of craven terror—of an intense and hopeless despair.
Did he live his life again in every detail of desire,
temptation, and surrender during that supreme moment of complete knowledge? He cried in a whisper
at some image, at some vision—he cried out twice, a
cry that was no more than a breath—

"'The horror! The horror!'

"I blew the candle out and left the cabin. The pilgrims were dining in the mess-room, and I took my
place opposite the manager, who lifted his eyes to give
me a questioning glance, which I successfully ignored.
He leaned back, serene, with that peculiar smile of his
sealing the unexpressed depths of his meanness. A
continuous shower of small flies streamed upon the
lamp, upon the cloth, upon our hands and faces. Suddenly the manager's boy put his insolent black head in
the doorway, and said in a tone of scathing contempt—

"'Mistah Kurtz—he dead.'

"All the pilgrims rushed out to see. I remained, and
went on with my dinner. I believe I was considered
brutally callous. However, I did not eat much. There
was a lamp in there—light, don't you know—and outside
it was so beastly, beastly dark. I went no more near the
remarkable man who had pronounced a judgment
upon the adventures of his soul on this earth. The
voice was gone. What else had been there? But I am
of course aware that next day the pilgrims buried
something in a muddy hole.

"And then they very nearly buried me.

"However, as you see, I did not go to join Kurtz there and then. I did not. I remained to dream the nightmare out to the end, and to show my loyalty to Kurtz once more. Destiny. My destiny! Droll thing life is—that mysterious arrangement of merciless logic for a futile purpose. The most you can hope from it is some knowledge of yourself—that comes too late—a crop of unextinguishable regrets. I have wrestled with death. It is the most unexciting contest you can imagine. It takes place in an impalpable grayness, with nothing underfoot, with nothing around, without spectators, without clamour, without glory, without the great desire of victory, without the great fear of defeat, in a sickly atmosphere of tepid scepticism, without much belief in your own right, and still less in that of your adversary. If such is the form of ultimate wisdom, then life is a greater riddle than some of us think it to be. I was within a hair's breadth of the last opportunity for pronouncement, and I found with humiliation that probably I would have nothing to say. This is the reason why I affirm that Kurtz was a remarkable man. He had something to say. He said it. Since I had peeped over the edge myself, I understand better the meaning of his stare, that could not see the flame of the candle, but was wide enough to embrace the whole universe, piercing enough to penetrate all the hearts that beat in the darkness. He had summed up —he had judged. 'The horror!' He was a remarkable man. After all, this was the expression of some sort of belief; it had candour, it had conviction, it had a vibrating note of revolt in its whisper, it had the appalling face of a glimpsed truth—the strange commingling of desire and hate. And it is not my own extremity

I remember best—a vision of grayness without form filled with physical pain, and a careless contempt for the evanescence of all things—even of this pain itself. No! It is his extremity that I seem to have lived through. True, he had made that last stride, he had stepped over the edge, while I had been permitted to draw back my hesitating foot. And perhaps in this is the whole difference; perhaps all the wisdom, and all truth, and all sincerity, are just compressed into that inappreciable moment of time in which we step over the threshold of the invisible. Perhaps! I like to think my summing-up would not have been a word of careless contempt. Better his cry—much better. It was an affirmation, a moral victory paid for by innumerable defeats, by abominable terrors, by abominable satisfactions. But it was a victory! That is why I have remained loyal to Kurtz to the last, and even beyond, when a long time after I heard once more, not his own voice, but the echo of his magnificent eloquence thrown to me from a soul as translucently pure as a cliff of crystal.

"No, they did not bury me, though there is a period of time which I remember mistily, with a shuddering wonder, like a passage through some inconceivable world that had no hope in it and no desire. I found myself back in the sepulchral city resenting the sight of people hurrying through the streets to filch a little money from each other, to devour their infamous cookery, to gulp their unwholesome beer, to dream their insignificant and silly dreams. They trespassed upon my thoughts. They were intruders whose knowledge of life was to me an irritating pretence, because I felt so sure they could not possibly know the things

I knew. Their bearing, which was simply the bearing
of commonplace individuals going about their business
in the assurance of perfect safety, was offensive to me
like the outrageous flauntings of folly in the face of
a danger it is unable to comprehend. I had no particular desire to enlighten them, but I had some difficulty in restraining myself from laughing in their
faces, so full of stupid importance. I daresay I was
not very well at that time. I tottered about the streets
—there were various affairs to settle—grinning bitterly
at perfectly respectable persons. I admit my behaviour
was inexcusable, but then my temperature was seldom
normal in these days. My dear aunt's endeavours to
'nurse up my strength' seemed altogether beside the
mark. It was not my strength that wanted nursing. it
was my imagination that wanted soothing. I kept the
bundle of papers given me by Kurtz, not knowing
exactly what to do with it. His mother had died lately,
watched over, as I was told, by his Intended. A clean-
shaved man, with an official manner and wearing gold-
rimmed spectacles, called on me one day and made in-
quiries, at first circuitous, afterwards suavely pressing,
about what he was pleased to denominate certain
'documents.' I was not surprised, because I had had
two rows with the manager on the subject out there.
I had refused to give up the smallest scrap out of that
package, and I took the same attitude with the spec-
tacled man. He became darkly menacing at last, and
with much heat argued that the Company had the right
to every bit of information about its 'territories.' And
said he, 'Mr. Kurtz's knowledge of unexplored regions
must have been necessarily extensive and peculiar—
owing to his great abilities and to the deplorable

circumstances in which he had been placed: therefore——' I assured him that Mr. Kurtz's knowledge,
however extensive, did not bear upon the problems of
commerce or administration. He invoked then the
name of science. 'It would be an incalculable loss if,'
etc., etc. I offered him the report on the 'Suppression
of Savage Customs,' with the postcriptum torn off. He
took it up eagerly, but ended by sniffing at it with an
air of contempt. 'This is not what we had a right to
expect,' he remarked. 'Expect nothing else,' I said.
'There are only private letters.' He withdrew upon
some threat of legal proceedings, and I saw him no
more; but another fellow, calling himself Kurtz's
cousin, appeared two days later, and was anxious to
hear all the details about his dear relative's last moments. Incidentally he gave me to understand that
Kurtz had been essentially a great musician. 'There
was the making of an immense success,' said the man,
who was an organist, I believe, with lank gray hair
flowing over a greasy coat-collar. I had no reason to
doubt his statement; and to this day I am unable to say
which was Kurtz's profession, whether he ever had any
—which was the greatest of his talents. I had taken him
for a painter who wrote for the papers, or else for a
journalist who could paint—but even the cousin (who
took snuff during the interview) could not tell me what
he had been—exactly. He was a universal genius—on
that point I agreed with the old chap, who thereupon
blew his nose noisily into a large cotton handkerchief
and withdrew in senile agitation, bearing off some
family letters and memoranda without importance.
Ultimately a journalist anxious to know something of
the fate of his 'dear colleague' turned up. This visitor

informed me Kurtz's proper sphere ought to have been politics 'on the popular side.' He had furry straight eyebrows, bristly hair cropped short, an eye-glass on a broad ribbon, and, becoming expansive, confessed his opinion that Kurtz really couldn't write a bit—'but heavens! how that man could talk. He electrified large meetings. He had faith—don't you see?—he had the faith. He could get himself to believe anything—anything. He would have been a splendid leader of an extreme party.' 'What party?' I asked. 'Any party,' answered the other. 'He was an—an—extremist.' Did I not think so? I assented. Did I know, he asked, with a sudden flash of curiosity, 'what it was that induced him to go out there?' 'Yes,' said I, and forthwith handed him the famous Report for publication, if he thought fit. He glanced through it hurriedly, mumbling all the time, judged 'it would do,' and took himself off with this plunder.

"Thus I was left at last with a slim packet of letters and the girl's portrait. She struck me as beautiful—I mean she had a beautiful expression. I know that the sunlight can be made to lie, too, yet one felt that no manipulation of light and pose could have conveyed the delicate shade of truthfulness upon those features. She seemed ready to listen without mental reservation, without suspicion, without a thought for herself. I concluded I would go and give her back her portrait and those letters myself. Curiosity? Yes; and also some other feeling perhaps. All that had been Kurtz's had passed out of my hands: his soul, his body, his station, his plans, his ivory, his career. There remained only his memory and his Intended—and I wanted to give that up, too, to the past, in a way—to surrender personally all that remained of him with me to that oblivion which is the last word of our common fate. I don't defend myself. I had no clear perception of what it was I really wanted. Perhaps it was an impulse of unconscious loyalty, or the fulfilment of one of those ironic necessities that lurk in the facts of human existence. I don't know. I can't tell. But I went.

"I thought his memory was like the other memories of the dead that accumulate in every man's life—a vague impress on the brain of shadows that had fallen on it in their swift and final passage; but before the high and ponderous door, between the tall houses of a street as still and decorous as a well-kept alley in a cemetery, I had a vision of him on the stretcher, opening his mouth voraciously, as if to devour all the earth with all its mankind. He lived then before me; he lived as much as he had ever lived—a shadow insatiable of splendid appearances, of frightful realities; a shadow darker than the shadow of the night, and draped nobly in the folds of gorgeous eloquence. The vision seemed to enter the house with me—the stretcher, the phantom-bearers, the wild crowd of obedient worshippers, the gloom of the forests, the glitter of the reach between the murky bends, the beat of the drum, regular and muffled like the beating of a heart—the heart of a conquering darkness. It was a moment of triumph for the wilderness, an invading and vengeful rush which, it seemed to me, I would have to keep back alone for the salvation of another soul. And the memory of what I had heard him say afar there, with the horned shapes stirring at my back, in the glow of fires, within the patient woods, those broken phrases came back to me, were heard again in their ominous and terrifying simplicity. I remembered his abject pleading, his abject threats, the colossal scale of his vile desires, the meanness, the torment, the tempestuous anguish of his soul. And later on I seemed to see his collected languid manner, when he said one day, 'This lot of ivory now is really mine. The Company did not pay for it. I collected it myself at a very great personal risk. I am afraid they will try to claim it as theirs though. H'm. It is a difficult case. What do you think I ought to do—resist? Eh? I want no more than justice.' . . . He wanted no more than justice—no more than justice. I rang the bell before a mahogany door on the first floor, and while I waited he seemed to stare at me out of the glassy panel—stare with that wide and immense stare embracing, condemning, loathing all the universe. I seemed to hear the whispered cry, 'The horror! The horror!'

"The dusk was falling. I had to wait in a lofty drawing-room with three long windows from floor to ceiling that were like three luminous and bedraped columns. The bent gilt legs and backs of the furniture shone in indistinct curves. The tall marble fireplace had a cold and monumental whiteness. A grand piano stood massively in a corner; with dark gleams on the flat surfaces like a sombre and polished sarcophagus. A high door opened—closed. I rose.

"She came forward, all in black, with a pale head, floating towards me in the dusk. She was in mourning. It was more than a year since his death, more than a year since the news came; she seemed as though she would remember and mourn for ever. She took both my hands in hers and murmured, 'I had heard you were coming.' I noticed she was not very young—I mean not girlish. She had a mature capacity for fidelity, for belief, for suffering. The room seemed to have grown darker, as if all the sad light of the cloudy evening had taken refuge on her forehead. This fair hair, this pale visage, this pure brow, seemed surrounded by an ashy halo from which the dark eyes looked out at me. Their glance was guileless, profound, confident, and trustful. She carried her sorrowful head as though she were proud of that sorrow, as though she would say, I—I alone know how to mourn for him as he deserves. But while we were still shaking hands, such a look of awful desolation came upon her face that I perceived she was one of those creatures that are not the playthings of Time. For her he had died only yesterday. And, by Jove! the impression was so powerful that for me, too, he seemed to have died only yesterday—nay, this very minute. I saw her and him in the same instant of time—his death and her sorrow—I saw her sorrow in the very moment of his death. Do you understand? I saw them together—I heard them together. She had said, with a deep catch of the breath, 'I have survived' while my strained ears seemed to hear distinctly, mingled with her tone of despairing regret, the summing up whisper of his eternal condemnation. I asked myself what I was doing there, with a sensation of panic in my heart as though I had blundered into a place of cruel and absurd mysteries not fit for a human being to behold. She motioned me to a chair. We sat down. I laid the packet gently on the little table, and she put her hand over it. . . . 'You knew him well,' she murmured, after a moment of mourning silence.

"'Intimacy grows quickly out there,' I said. 'I knew

✗ him as well as it is possible for one man to know another.'

" 'And you admired him,' she said. 'It was impossible to know him and not to admire him. Was it?'

" 'He was a remarkable man,' I said, unsteadily. Then before the appealing fixity of her gaze, that seemed to watch for more words on my lips, I went on, 'It was impossible not to——'

" 'Love him,' she finished eagerly, silencing me into an appalled dumbness. 'How true! how true! But when you think that no one knew him so well as I! I had all his noble confidence. I knew him best.'

" 'You knew him best,' I repeated. And perhaps she did. But with every word spoken the room was growing darker, and only her forehead, smooth and white, remained illumined by the unextinguishable light of belief and love.

" 'You were his friend,' she went on. 'His friend,' she repeated, a little louder. 'You must have been, if he had given you this, and sent you to me. I feel I can speak to you—and oh! I must speak. I want you—you who have heard his last words—to know I have been worthy of him. . . . It is not pride. . . . Yes! I am proud to know I understood him better than any one on earth—he told me so himself. And since his mother died I have had no one—no one—to—to——'

"I listened. The darkness deepened. I was not even sure whether he had given me the right bundle. I rather suspect he wanted me to take care of another batch of his papers which, after his death, I saw the manager examining under the lamp. And the girl talked, easing her pain in the certitude of my sympathy; she talked as thirsty men drink. I had heard that her engagement with Kurtz had been disapproved by her people. He wasn't rich enough or something. And indeed I don't know whether he had not been a pauper all his life. He had given me some reason to infer that it was his impatience of comparative poverty that drove him out there.

"'. . . Who was not his friend who had heard him speak once?' she was saying. 'He drew men towards him by what was best in them.' She looked at me with intensity. 'It is the gift of the great,' she went on, and the sound of her low voice seemed to have the accompaniment of all the other sounds, full of mystery, desolation, and sorrow, I had ever heard—the ripple of the river, the soughing of the trees swayed by the wind, the murmurs of the crowds, the faint ring of incomprehensible words cried from afar, the whisper of a voice speaking from beyond the threshold of an eternal darkness. 'But you have heard him! You know!' she cried.

"'Yes, I know,' I said with something like despair in my heart, but bowing my head before the faith that was in her, before that great and saving illusion that shone with an unearthly glow in the darkness, in the triumphant darkness from which I could not have defended her—from which I could not even defend myself.

"'What a loss to me—to us!'—she corrected herself with beautiful generosity; then added in a murmur, 'To the world.' By the last gleams of twilight I could see the glitter of her eyes, full of tears—of tears that would not fall.

"'I have been very happy—very fortunate—very

proud,' she went on. 'Too fortunate. Too happy for a little while. And now I am unhappy for—for life.'

"She stood up; her fair hair seemed to catch all the remaining light in a glimmer of gold. I rose, too.

"'And of all this,' she went on, mournfully, 'of all his promise, and of all his greatness, of his generous mind, of his noble heart, nothing remains—nothing but a memory. You and I——'

"'We shall always remember him,' I said, hastily.

"'No!' she cried. 'It is impossible that all this should be lost—that such a life should be sacrificed to leave nothing—but sorrow. You know what vast plans he had. I knew of them, too—I could not perhaps understand—but others knew of them. Something must remain. His words, at least, have not died.'

"'His words will remain,' I said.

"'And his example,' she whispered to herself. 'Men looked up to him—his goodness shone in every act. His example——'

"'True,' I said; 'his example, too. Yes, his example. I forgot that.'

"'But I do not. I cannot—I cannot believe—not yet. I cannot believe that I shall never see him again, that nobody will see him again, never, never, never.'

"She put out her arms as if after a retreating figure, stretching them back and with clasped pale hands across the fading and narrow sheen of the window. Never see him! I saw him clearly enough then. I shall see this eloquent phantom as long as I live, and I shall see her, too, a tragic and familiar Shade, resembling in this gesture another one, tragic also, and bedecked with powerless charms, stretching bare brown arms over the glitter of the infernal stream, the stream of darkness. She said suddenly very low, 'He died as he lived.'

" 'His end,' said I, with dull anger stirring in me, 'was in every way worthy of his life.'

" 'And I was not with him,' she murmured. My anger subsided before a feeling of infinite pity.

" 'Everything that could be done——' I mumbled.

" 'Ah, but I believed in him more than any one on earth—more than his own mother, more than—himself. He needed me! Me! I would have treasured every sigh, every word, every sign, every glance.'

"I felt like a chill grip on my chest. 'Don't,' I said, in a muffled voice.

" 'Forgive me. I—I—have mourned so long in silence —in silence. . . . You were with him—to the last? I think of his loneliness. Nobody near to understand him as I would have understood. Perhaps no one to hear. . . .'

" 'To the very end,' I said, shakily. 'I heard his very last words. . . .' I stopped in a fright.

" 'Repeat them,' she murmured in a heartbroken tone. 'I want—I want—something—something—to—to live with.' *Marlow ~~also~~ lies*

"I was on the point of crying at her, 'Don't you hear them?' The dusk was repeating them in a persistent whisper all around us, in a whisper that seemed to swell menacingly like the first whisper of a rising wind. 'The horror! the horror!'

" 'His last word—to live with,' she insisted. 'Don't you understand I loved him—I loved him—I loved him!'

"I pulled myself together and spoke slowly.

" 'The last word he pronounced was—your name.'

"I heard a light sigh and then my heart stood still, stopped dead short by an exulting and terrible cry,

by the cry of inconceivable triumph and of unspeakable pain. 'I knew it—I was sure!' . . . She knew. She
was sure. I heard her weeping; she had hidden her
face in her hands. It seemed to me that the house
would collapse before I could escape, that the heavens
would fall upon my head. But nothing happened. The
heavens do not fall for such a trifle. Would they have
fallen, I wonder, if I had rendered Kurtz that justice
which was his due? Hadn't he said he wanted only
justice? But I couldn't. I could not tell her. It would
have been too dark—too dark altogether. . . ."

Marlow ceased, and sat apart, indistinct and silent,
in the pose of a meditating Buddha. Nobody moved for
a time. "We have lost the first of the ebb," said the
Director, suddenly. I raised my head. The offing was
barred by a black bank of clouds, and the tranquil
waterway leading to the uttermost ends of the earth
flowed sombre under an overcast sky—seemed to lead
into the heart of an immense darkness.